PORTER ROCKWELL,
IKE POTTER:
HEROES OR VILLAINS

BILL KID

Order this book online at www.trafford.com
or email orders@trafford.com

Most Trafford titles are also available at major online book retailers.

Printed in the United States of America.

ISBN: 978-1-4669-7502-6 (sc)
ISBN: 978-1-4669-7501-9 (hc)
ISBN: 978-1-4669-7500-2 (e)

Library of Congress Control Number: 2012924332

Trafford rev. 02/04/2013

 www.trafford.com

North America & international
toll-free: 1 888 232 4444 (USA & Canada)
phone: 250 383 6864 ♦ fax: 812 355 4082

CONTENTS

MORNING RIDE

Porter rose one morning early. He wanted to ride down and take a look at the new arrivals in Springville. It was a bright, beautiful day. The sun was just touching the plants and buildings with an orange tint and it was breath taking. Porter Rockwell wondered if he had ever seen a more beautiful morning. Porter smiled to himself thinking how many people thought what a tough hombre he was and here he was thinking how beautiful the morning was. Maybe it was the softness that Joseph had taught him about loving his neighbor, but nonetheless Porter knew he could do what needed to be done. He had come from a timid farm boy in New York to one of the most capable men in the west. He wasn't one to brag but he knew there would be times in the future when he would be called upon to go after a rustler or some other outlaw and he knew he would do it. He had come a long way from that scared young man roped in that outhouse after he had peed down his leg in Missouri. He would be forever grateful to Sylvester for training him to become the capable gun hand he now was. Sylvester had almost killed him trying to drive him off the first day he met him. Port was insistent he teach him what he knew, but

Sylvester was not easily convinced that he was teachable. After he took bullets from Sylvester's gun, one in the leg and one in the shoulder and told him his story about being roped in the outhouse and his accident down his leg when he was at the height of embarrassment and had no self- confidence, the gunfighter finally softened. Sylvester and his wife nursed him back to health and then the training began.[1] That was an experience he would never forget. He had gained the confidence to handle just about anything required, but he still hated it when men drew their guns or resisted being taken in. That meant that he would have to kill them and that was never his first choice.

Porter saddled his favorite horse. Hondo was a tall sorrel. He was at least 16 hands high and he could move. Porter knew he had to be ready when he hit the saddle or Hondo might leave him in the dust. Hondo was always ready to move and move quickly. That was what he liked about him. There were times when that quick movement would save the lives of both Hondo and him.

Porter arrived in Springville mid-morning and the new settlers were unpacking their wagons. Porter didn't want to have conversations with many of them. Porter was set in his ways and he didn't find every man's conversation worth the effort. He liked to size up men. He had a good eye for what men were all about with few words being said; how a man moved, the sureness he had in his stride, the shortness he

---

[1] Storm Testament 6, Rockwell, Lee Nelson, p. 77-90

had with his family and his animals. How a man treated his animals told him volumes about what a man was all about. Many times Port had chastised men for poor treatment of animals. Porter remembered what Joseph had said about there being a day when we would be able to talk to our animals. He knew that day wouldn't be tomorrow, but far into the future. He never wanted an animal to chastise him for poor treatment. Seriously, Port loved animals and knew each one of them played a part in the scheme of things and he appreciated each part they played.

One family caught his eye and he stopped his horse nearby to listen to them talking. He liked what he heard. Far too many young people showed little if any respect for their parents and he liked what he was hearing.

"Son, would you mind taking that horse tack over there by that tree", said the man. "Dad, I have a feeling that is where you are thinking of building the barn," said the young man.

"I totally agree, the shade of that tree will be perfect,"

"I'm glad you approve," said the man. "Ike, you know you need to start thinking soon of a wife." "Brigham is portioning out the lots based on how large your family is and right now you get nothing,"

"I know Dad, but that is not something I want to rush into,"

"But the quicker you marry the better chance I have of having you close. The lots will go fast,"

"Dad, I understand what you are saying and I will. I will start looking around. I have already seen some pretty girls over by that wagon," said the young man.

The two men sparked Port's interest and he had to know their names. He rode by another wagon close by.

"Howdy," said Port. "How was your trip?" said Port.

"Howdy, my name is Bill White. That trip is not something I want to do for some time. It was hell. The miles went on forever."

"Hey, did you catch the names of this family over here," said Porter.

"I did. That is Ransom Potter and his son Ike," explained Bill. "They are a hard working family. I never heard them complain the whole trip. They helped us whenever we needed help. I look forward to them as neighbors."

"We can use as many hard workers as we can find," commented Port. "This is tough country and we still have a lot to do. You have a great day and good luck with that storm I see coming. You might want to get your stock together."

Porter lightly touched Hondo with his spurs and rode off. He never liked to hit his horse too hard with them. He wouldn't want anyone spurring him hard. He had a little time before he had to get back and he rode up the canyon to the east of Springville for a while. It seemed he could never get enough of this new land. He was thinking seriously of going out where there weren't so many people and homesteading a section. The only trouble was Brigham wanted him close in case there was any trouble. Some day he would find the time. Some day he would make the time. As he rode his thoughts returned to that young man and his father. What were their names again? Ransom and Ike Potter was what Bill had said. Porter thought he would keep an eye on them. There was something about them that he liked. He couldn't put his finger on it. Maybe it was the respect and the eagerness to work he liked. Well, he thought, time will tell. This country might try all of us before we are through.

THE TALL SORREL

Ike had noticed the man on that tall sorrel and wondered who he was. He strode over to Bill White.

"Howdy Bill, I saw you talking to a man on a good looking sorrel a few minutes ago. Did you catch his name," said Ike.

"You wouldn't know a good looking sorrel if it walked up and stepped on you."

"You know Bill, some day you are going to give me too hard of a time and I will have to knock you upside the head."

"Do you suppose I will lose any sleep tonight worrying about that happening. I could beat you with one hand tied behind my back."

"Someday we will have to find out who of us is the tougher. You might have your hands full of trouble with me."

Ike knew it would never come to that. He liked Bill. There was no getting around that.

"Now, about that good looking sorrel I was talking about."

"You know, he didn't seem eager to tell me his name, but I have an idea that was Porter Rockwelll."

"You mean THE Porter Rockwell. The bodyguard for Joseph and now Brigham. No, it couldn't be," said Ike. "How could we be lucky enough to run into that guy the first day here.

"If that was him, I can see why he wasn't in a hurry to say his name. I'm sure he has his hands full with admirers or enemies depending on who the people are," said Ike.

"He was asking about you and your father," explained Bill.

"He seemed quite interested in you two. I can't see how anyone could be interested in you two. You are two of the orneriest cusses I have ever seen. "said Bill.

"You keep giving me a hard time and I'll get worse everyday Bill," responded Ike.

Ike liked Bill. He knew he had a friend for life if he took care of that relationship. Bill was just that kind of a guy. That kind of a guy is hard to find and he knew he would do all he could do to keep him as a friend.

As Ike walked back to where his father was working he thought about Porter Rockwell. What a life he had led. It was said he had killed one hundred men. He didn't look like a cruel kind of a guy. Ike wondered what he was like. He decided he would try to get to know him and the last thing he ever wanted to do was make him mad at him. He had an idea that that was one tough hombre. He hoped he had a joking side. Ike had a knack about joking with people. He had made many a friend joking around with them. Joshing people was always fun unless you took it too far and he had learned when that was enough. Sometimes he kidded too much, but if he did he was always ready to set it straight and not have anyone's feelings hurt.

Ike started thinking seriously about a wife. He knew it would be to his advantage in terms of land to have more than one wife since polygamy was now being practiced. But he thought, better worry about the first one first and he planned to pick well. There appeared to be so many young girls here in Springville that choosing might be hard. He knew what he wanted his wife to be like and he planned to keep that in mind as he looked. Let's see, he wanted her to have a sense of humor, be hard working, but know when to have fun to. He wanted her to like the mountains as he did.

He had never seen more beautiful mountains than right here especially to the east of Springville. They were something to behold. He had noticed as they had come into the area all of the mountains to the east and they just seemed to go on forever. None of them bored him. He thought he could ride forever in there and never see the same place again. He hadn't seen a lot of game though. He had heard that the whites hadn't been too careful in killing them. He had always been told by his father how the Indians had been much better at preserving the game supply. Ransom had said the Indians never killed more than was needed for meat and supplies. But the talk here was whites had killed some of the game just so the Indians would starve and would be eager to move on. That rubbed Ike the wrong way and he wanted to see if that was true. He didn't like to take anyone's opinion solely on what was said. He knew it was always better to find out for yourself.

So what was he thinking about when the mountains distracted him. Oh, yeah, a wife. The thought scarred him a little. He had heard of some divorces and that wasn't what he wanted any part of. Even THE Porter Rockwell had been divorced by his first wife and he thought if a man that capable could lose a wife any of us could. His mom and dad had made a go of marriage and he never could see them splitting up, so he guessed he would take a chance at it too. What scarred him most about it was all the things he wanted to do. Would a wife get bored with him being gone so much? Would she want to leave? Hmm, too many worries, he decided he would take a chance and marry.

Right now that would have to wait. He and his dad had a cabin to build and corrals to build and a barn. It would be fun. Ike was old enough to enjoy working with his hands. He loved to work hard and see the things grow from the ground up. It was a great feeling to see things form from things that you could find in these mountains, logs for the cabin, poles for the corrals and the barn too. He wondered how many things he would build in his life. That was how a man left his mark, what he built with his own two hands and the friends he made. He thought jokingly, what was more important, buildings or friends? He knew the answer to that easily. He had heard Joseph say many times that the second greatest commandment was to love your neighbors as yourself and already in life he could see how that paid off. Friends like Bill White were forever and more. He had heard his dad say that good friends were not only for this life but for the next one too. His dad believed our friends will be our friends through the eternities. That was an exciting thought to think friends were always ours if we treated them right.

THE MOUNTAINS

Oh, how Porter loved to ride in the mountains. He would rather be in the mountains then just about anything he could think of. It was spring and the trees were just leafing out. It was such a beautiful sight. The grass was just beginning to poke its little noses out of the ground. The air was crisp and clean. He could smell the sage in his nostrils. Some people didn't appreciate the smell of sage, but he wasn't one of them. He loved the smell, especially after a rain. The sky was a beautiful blue with white wisps of clouds here and there. He couldn't imagine a more beautiful day.

Just then he noticed a different smell and he knew what it was. He could often smell elk before he saw them or heard them. Four head of elk moved on his right through the trees. He knew there were probably more back in the trees. They were probably the biggest reason he enjoyed the mountains so much. He loved to run into elk. He also preferred their meat to beef. He loved to sit down to an elk steak and enjoy the rich flavor. He wasn't seeing as many elk or deer as he had seen when he first came to the valley. He often heard men talking about shooting elk and deer just to help remove the Indian problem. He thought to himself, the Indians weren't the problem, we were. Here was a culture that had been here for thousands of years, maintaining the balance of nature, living off the land, but never ruining all that we see and along come the white man and ravishes the land like tomorrow doesn't matter. Tomorrow does matter. We have children and grandchildren who will want this land just as we found it and I doubt that we will leave it as we found it. Already we are killing to many elk and deer, cutting down the forests, building roads, building canals, building towns, changing everything that once was. Changing everything that the Indian holds sacred. Who is right? Who says we have a right to change the face of land and boot off the people that loved this land as it was for centuries. Who gave us the right, "Manifest Destiny", hah. That is just an excuse to do whatever we want.

It wasn't smart for him to think that way. There were very few of his friends and neighbors that think that way. He needed to keep that kind of thinking to himself. Sometimes he found himself in groups that wouldn't appreciate his thoughts at all. But Porter was a man who cared little what others thought. Nothing could change his doubts that the red man wasn't being treated right. Good old "Manifest Destiny" had pushed the Indians back all across the west. How far would we push them until they fell into the sea? Each time we pushed them we promised them things, little or none of which they received. That was an interesting thought. That means that every time we made them promises and didn't keep them, we were lying and we call ourselves a righteous people. He had never known an Indian to lie. He had never heard of an Indian lying. A large part of their culture was to keep their word no matter what. That's interesting. Port began to laugh so hard he almost fell of Hondo and he scarred the elk away. They were all gone in maybe 20 seconds. Oh how he loved those animals. He could never kill one except for food. He loved them more than himself.

His thoughts returned to why he had almost fallen off Hondo, then he remembered. We lie to the Indians knowing we will never keep the agreements we make and we pat ourselves on the back about how righteous we are. Maybe we are the people that have a long way to go. Maybe when we get to the Pearly Gates we will have to step aside and let the Indians go in. Interesting thought, huh.

Well he had done it. His big mouth had chased away the most beautiful animals in the whole world. He relaxed, knowing there would be another time when he would see elk. He hoped those clowns who shot elk to starve the Indians would realize what they were doing before it was too late and leave us with little or no elk and deer. He relaxed and thought about what a beautiful sight that was too see that little herd of elk. What a joy to see the beauty this land offered.

There he was again, thinking of beauty when he was considered a hard man to deal with. But he couldn't deny it. He loved beautiful things. As he rode along, he thought about the day he had met Luana. She was a sight to behold. She was probably the prettiest girl he had ever seen and he had been so lucky to have her hand in marriage. They had had 4 children together. Sometimes he missed her and he missed her beauty, but truly beauty is only skin deep. It had seemed like no matter what he had done to please her, it was never enough. He remembered the day he had turned over his guns to the Missourians how upset she was, she was beside herself not understanding why I had given up my gun. I had been a hard thing, but all two hundred of our group had agreed it was better to have peace than to have a war. Of course, later on, the Missourians had taken full advantage of that. When the mobs began to attack, the Mormons had no way to defend themselves.

As he rode along he remembered the day he had heard about Luana. He had met Williard Sweeney and he talked about her non-stop. He had described her to the point that he wanted to meet her. He had spent hours thinking about her and was going to see her when he ran into Sweeney on the road. When Sweeney had heard of his intentions they had raced their horses with the winner getting to go to Luana's and the loser going home. Sweeney's gloating attitude had cost him his date with Luana that day and awarded Port the opportunity to finally meet Luana. He had never been able to make Luana happy after their marriage. As he thought he realized his habit of not sharing what was on his mind or his long absences must have played a part in the marriage's demise.

A WIFE

Ransom and Ike began first on the cabin. They couldn't get very far on it until they had to work at getting crops planted. The winter would be here too soon and they needed food for that. Their good looks wouldn't feed them too long. Ike loved to turn the ground over. He loved the look of the soil as it turned. It looked so black until the wind and the sun touched it and turned it a much lighter brown. As he turned the ground over the seagulls would swoop down and eat whatever they could scavenge. He wondered how they lasted in the winter. He had heard that birds don't worry about raiment and food that God takes care of them. Wouldn't that be nice, but he knew he better do his part or God wouldn't take care of him. The nice thing about getting the ground ready to plant, there was a lot of time to think. And once again he was thinking about a wife. He thought maybe today after work he would go meet some of the local girls.

That night he cleaned up and walked around talking to young people about his age. It seemed like most of the girls talked about things he had no interest in. How it was hard in the hot sun to keep their hair nice and how the wind blew and made a mess of it. They talked of how much they hoped their father would get some more money so they could get that new dress they had seen in the catalog. Ike thought he wanted his wife to feel it was important to look nice, but he felt like most of the girls were obsessed by looking nice. That night he came around a corner and there were three attractive girls. He thought the one was especially nice looking. He walked on by and smiled at them. They all three smiled back. He went on a little further and saw some boys.

"Hi gents," said Ike. "Nice night, huh. Do you know who those three girls I just passed are?"

"Nice looking girls aren't they," said the taller boy. "We are trying to get up enough nerve to go talk to them. We have been looking at them for the longest time and they keep giving us the eye, but here we stand. Sometimes it's hard to start a conversation with girls. If they start talking about shoes and their hair, then what do we say. It's a hard thing, don't you think?"

"But there are so many things to talk about," said Ike. "If they talk about things you don't want to talk about, change the subject. Us men don't have to let the women of our world force us to think like they do. If they don't want to hear about the important things in life then they aren't for you anyhow. That's how I see it," said Ike.

"You know I never thought about it that way," said the tall youth. "So the trick is to force them to talk about horses, cows, corrals, and fishing. Is that right?"

"Well, young man, I wouldn't put it quite like that. If you force a girl to do anything you will probably spend your life alone. You have to be nice and not let her know you are changing the subject. The trick is to be tricky, get that," said Ike.

"Nah, I'm not sure I will ever figure women out," said the youth.

The boys said they were all sisters and they were nice. He walked back and started talking to them. He turned to the boys and raised his arms as if to say, see it isn't hard, just do it. The one that had caught his eye said her name was Mary and he hardly heard what the others said. He thought that he wanted to get to know her. After talking for a while he asked if he could walk with her and since it wasn't too late she consented to walk.

As they walked he thought, he liked the way she walked and talked and most of all she wasn't like the other girls he had met who were so concerned about their hair and other menial things. She wanted to talk about what was in the mountains and the animals that could be found there. She talked also about the plight of the Indians. This had been their land and now whose land was it. Whoever could force others off?

"For what, centuries, the Indians have had this land. I heard some of the men talking and they said that it is okay whatever they do to the Indians because they have done it to each other for years," said Mary. "When they talk like that it makes sense, but somehow it is still wrong to come here and do what we are doing. My father said, that as the frontier moved steadily west we made many agreements with the Indians and we have not kept one of them. Every time the whites failed to deliver all that they had promised. Sometimes it was money, sometimes it was food, blankets, things they needed and every time they had lied and never planned to complete the bargain. I read the other night something an Indian had written and it said the Indians could never believe that the white man could lie. That is something that I just can't accept. Our parents teach us to never lie and yet we live with a lie every day," said Mary.

"Mary, you are scaring me. Everything you are saying is the very things I have been thinking about all my life. I had some Indian friends back east before we came out and they are people. They are no different than you and me. Sure they wear their hair different and they have different customs, but they are just like you and me. I think they are more honorable than some whites, maybe most whites," said Ike. "I suggest you be very careful or I might like you too much. But I have to go now. Dad and I have an early start tomorrow. We decided to work for a couple of hours on the cabin and then spend the rest of the day planting and plowing. It all needs to happen. Can I see you again? I really enjoyed our talk and I am looking forward to talking again real soon. Could I meet you here tomorrow night, say the same time."

"I think that could be arranged. See you tomorrow night."

Ike hurried off. He liked to be dependable to his dad and he went right to bed. He loved working hard because he always slept well after. Tonight he didn't fall right to sleep. His mind was too full of Mary. Not only was she one of the prettiest girls he had ever seen, but what she talked about and what was important to her was exactly what Ike would want her to think. As Ike drifted off, all he thought about was Mary. What a lady!!!!

Ike woke early. His mom already had the fire going and had biscuits and jerky ready. Later they would be able to eat differently, but for now vegetables had to be grown, the cabin built, the barn up for the winter. There was so much to do. His dad had always taught him though that things that are worthwhile don't happen fast. They take time and half of the accomplishment is the journey, not necessarily the end result.

"How did you sleep, son", said his mom. "What time did you get to bed ? "I know how he slept," said his dad. "He snored so loud I didn't get any sleep. He will have to do most of the work now. He'll learn to stay up all night howling at the moon. If you dance all night you have to pay the fiddler. Did you get that wife found last night?"

"It's funny that you should ask, I think I did. Her name is Mary and she thinks so much like a wife should. She was so interesting to talk to. Everything that is important to me seemed to be important to her. It was so interesting to meet someone like her. But we will see, I won't jump early. Life is a long time, in fact, eternity is much longer. How have you and mom made such a good marriage, Dad."

"That is so easy to explain, son. Your mom says jump and I say, How high? Works every time. Can you see us getting anything done, building the cabin, getting the barn up and the fields plowed without her sayso?" said Ransom. "Couldn't be done. Does that help to understand the workings of a marriage?"

"Oh, by the way, I was in bed early" commented Ike. "When a man tells another man he will, then he does. Providing the creek doesn't rise and the good Lord is willing", said Ike.

"That's my son," said Ransom. "Taught him everything he knows."

"You did too good of a job of teaching him how to josh. It's getting harder and harder to tell when he is not kidding around. He's getting more and more like you every day, but I guess that is what I love about you two so much. Why don't you two get to work. What are you two going to get done standing around here all day," said Rhoda.

"See son, I told you how marriage works so let's get to it."

Ike had an older brother and sister and they were busy with their own lives. Frank was three years younger and he would be up soon to help. He was a lot of help but was a little slower getting going in the mornings. Ike was considered to be a man and was expected to do a man's share of the work. So after breakfast Ike concentrated on each step of building the cabin, the shaping of the logs and then using the horses to set the logs in place. Ike's father, Frank and he made good time that morning on the cabin. He could tell Ransom was enjoying his work. He guessed that was where he had learned to love working with his hands, from his dad. Frank was good help and he got a lot done for a teenager, but he didn't enjoy it as much as Ike and his dad. He didn't attack it with the same enthusiasm that Ike did. Ike wondered if Frank would grow out of his attitude. Some men never learned to like to work with their hands. More than one outlaw had chosen an easier way to live. Some men should never have been taught how to use a gun. For men like that maybe someday there would no guns in the west. Ike thought though he hoped that day never came. He always wanted to be able to defend his family if the need was there. They finished what they wanted to accomplish that morning and went back to plowing and getting ready to plant. It all had to happen about the same time to be ready for winter and winter always comes.

As Ike plowed it again gave him a chance to think about that girl that was always in his head now. Maybe he should never have met her then at least he could keep his head a little clearer. Females had a way of making your thoughts muddy and that is one thing a guy didn't need is unclear thoughts. Maybe God should have only put men on this earth in the consideration of clear thoughts. He always got a little silly when he was plowing, nothing else to do but think. As he thought about her, he thought about seeing her tonight. It was already four o'clock. The time would fly by and then he could see her again. Oh, there she is again, in his thoughts.

THE DATE

Ike was anxious to see Mary again. He hurried, cleaned up and took a little more time to look just right. He had never before been quite as much concerned about his appearance, but tonight was special. He was seeing the girl of his dreams. Darn those dreams. A man needs to keep a clear head and his head certainly wasn't clear.

They hadn't really agreed on a time, but he thought she would think the same time they had met the night before so he made sure he was there just a little early. He didn't want to spoil this night by being late. He was there only a few minutes when she came around the corner. He could tell by the light in her eyes that she liked him. They started talking almost immediately in the same place they had left off, the land, the mountains, the Indians, and the future of this valley.

"Did you know that Jim Bridger told Brigham Young that no one would raise crops in this valley before we started settling here. He said that crops, fruit trees and vegetable gardens wouldn't grow. Look how wrong he was. I can see why he would have thought that. I haven't been there yet, but I am told that the Salt Lake is so salty how could anything grow near to it. It makes perfect sense to me. But look what happens; crops, trees and vegetable gardens do great," said Ike. "Isn't it great. We finally found a place where no one can make us move. Mostly, because no one else wants it. It is a perfect home for the Mormons. No more Haun's Mill nonsense or the way we were treated in Nauvoo. But Nauvoo was a swamp and we drained it and made it beautiful. So, you never know, maybe they will find a way to drive us from this place to, even if," This is the Place,'" said Mary.

They both laughed. They both knew without saying that those were the words of Brigham Young when he first saw this valley at the head of Immigration Canyon. It seemed like so much of their communication was without words. It was almost as if they could read each other's thoughts. It was special to spend time together, to feel without saying. Ike doubted he could or would ever find another that he could feel about as he was starting to feel about Mary. She was a prize.

But tomorrow brought another morning and an early rise. He had to cut their date short even though he hated to. He kept thinking he could talk to her forever and never cover the same ground. Maybe even eternity. One thing they were learning in church was that death didn't end it all. That death was just a temporary change and that there was much more after that and that a man and a woman could do all there was to do after death together. Together, what a nice thought right now as he walked away from Mary. "Together", had such a nice ring. Ike thought, there I go again getting my brain all clouded. A man had too much to do and he didn't have time to have his head clouded. Women, that is one mistake the Lord made when he made this world. He smiled after thinking that, because he knew that women were what made this world special, cloudy heads or not.

The next morning Ransom and Ike worked on the cabin first. Ransom was starting to tighten up a little on Frank and he arrived minutes after they started.

"Frank, I'm going to be a little tougher than before on you," said Ike's dad. "You are becoming a man and therefore you will have mansize responsibilities. Is that okay with you? I wanted to get your opinion on that before we started doing it. I wanted to see how you feel about it. I feel that if I treat you like a man, you will like it better and not mind the change. Being treated like a man means a lot of benefits, but it also means more responsibilities. I think you know what I mean. You know I have been a little different with your brother here than you. I know you are still not quite as big as he is, but you are close. What do you think?"

"Schucks, dad. I can near whip Ike now, what are you talking about."

"Being near to whipping me is just a little bit different, right shorty," pushed Ike. "Come back in about a year and we will talk about it then. Hey, shorty, I would go for it if I were you. Being treated like a man is worth just about anything. Try it, you will like it."

"I will like it, thanks, dad," commented Frank.

What was different was Frank was given a little bit more respect than before. It wasn't a huge difference, but enough that if you looked for it, you could see it. It wasn't a huge difference. It was like taking a thirsty horse to water. If you give them to much they will founder and you may lose the horse.

Work went smoothly that morning and they accomplished a lot before knocking off for lunch and going back to the fields. Ike hitched up the team to the plow and began that job. There he was again, plowing and thinking about.... Mary. He couldn't seem to keep his mind off that girl. When they were building the cabin it was a little easier because the work took the concentration to do the work and not get hurt. When you were swinging an axe or setting logs, you better have your mind on what you are doing. More than one man has lost a finger or two not paying attention.

Mary and Ike started walking around town together holding hands. Ike loved the feel of Mary's hand in his. It was small and very comfortable. As he held her hand he felt feelings of always wanting to protect her. Protect from the world, Indians, anything that might hurt her in anyway. He had little time to do that except after work in the evenings. Ransom approved. He and mom had met Mary and they were excited about the prospects. Ike didn't care who saw them walking. He knew Elmer Judd liked her. He had heard rumors that he did. Rumors meant little to Ike. If Elmer didn't like it, he needed to talk to Ike himself, not ask his friends to give him a message.

Ike thought if he were to get started on his life and present himself to a father to earn the hand of a wife that he ought to see about some land of his own. He was old enough. He went to the Bishop who was the appropriator of the land.

"Bishop, I am old enough and I want to start a family. Could I request a piece of land and start a cabin and enough ground to raise some cows and crops," said Ike.

"Usually we wait until all the lads are already married and need to raise their families. Do you have someone in mind to marry? I notice you and Mary Ford are spending a lot of time together. Do you have her in mind for a wife?"

"Bishop, I want to prove what I can do before I ask a girl's father for her hand. I know, as a father, I would want to know that my daughter's suitor had the ability to take care of her. Just because a young fellow told me what he would do, I would want him to prove some things to me," commented Ike.

"I think Elmer might have Mary in mind for a wife. Since her father died, he has been planting their crops and helping her mom out. In fact I've heard that Elmer has his eye on her. So be careful, he has become somewhat of an influence since he built that big room on his house for dancing. That is not something a Bishop should be saying, but just a word to the wise," said the Bishop. "You know, I have been watching you and your dad working over at his place and I am pretty impressed. You are what I would call an enterprising young man and I believe in giving a leg up to young men such as you. How about that parcel over by your dad? If you become more enterprising and have more than one wife there is more land to the west of that. I am encouraging you to be careful of Elmer and don't prove me wrong. Let's see what you can do."

"Bishop, don't think for one minute you will be disappointed. I know what I can do and I will do it," said Ike.

So Ike had his work cut out for him. When he told his mom and dad they were going to be neighbors they were so excited.

"Son, that means you, Frank and I have a whole lot of work to do. We need to finish the cabin and it is close. We need to finish the barn and the corrals. Then we need to the same time get your cabin at least built before winter. We are going to be as busy as ants on an ant hill," said Ransom.

"Does that mean you are going to help me on my place?" returned Ike.

"That is a silly question, son."

JOSEPH

As he rode along back toward Salt Lake he thought about the first time he had met Joseph Smith and how they had become friends. The Smith and the Rockwell farms were close to one another. There had become a time when he would have done anything for that man and still would. His memories of Joseph were the best. Joseph had been 7 years older than him, but still had always treated him very well. Joseph had never forgotten their friendship in any way. Many times Joseph had helped him and many times Porter had helped Joseph. As kids they had had a common bond because both of them had a limp. When they were still children many nights found the Rockwells and the Smiths enjoying time together after the work of the day was over.

Later when they both had become men, Porter became a friend and a confidant of Joseph. Joseph had actually asked Porter to be his bodyguard and he worked at that for several years. After Joseph was martyred, Porter lost his best friend and said so many times. He had always felt that if he had been at the Carthage jail that day that things would have turned out differently. That maybe he would have somehow changed the killing of Joseph and Hyrum, that somehow he could have stopped their murder, that somehow he could have altered the stupidity of that day. How stupid it had been! How can a nation founded on the belief and the need to have freedom of religion be so impossible to deal with? Joseph had even gone to Washington D.C. to ask for relief from the mobs. He had been told by the United States President there was nothing that could be done. There was religious persecution at every turn. It had been the case in Palmyra, New York; Kirtland, Ohio; Jackson county; Missouri; Clay county, Missouri; Far West, Missouri; and then again in Nauvoo, Illinois. Finally, hopefully now they could be left alone. But that is what they thought when they drained the swamps in Nauvoo and built a beautiful town. Wow, when will this people be left alone.

Maybe that was part of the reason why Porter had such a soft spot for the Indians. We were doing exactly what had been done to the Mormons back east. It seems like people never learn. It seems like all people really only care about themselves. As much persecution as the Mormons had taken back east should have taught the Mormons total tolerance for all people, but when it came to the Indians they had no empathy. People are interesting. They were so upset at how they would move someplace, build homes and a town and then have to walk away from them and do the same thing the next place and then they get here and abuse the native people just as they had been abused back east. People never learn. I guess we expected the Indians to just get out of our way and let us have anything we wanted. Hmmm, just like the mobs in the east wanted. Not too many saw the parallel that he could so clearly see.

Porter had so many fond memories of Joseph Smith. He clearly remembered the day he had been with him on the streets of Nauvoo when two ruffians had accosted Joseph. Joseph had listened to their abusive remarks as long as he could, then grabbed one of them and shoved him against the wall. At that point a pistol was pulled and Porter was able to knock it to the side. Joseph may have been killed that day if Porter hadn't been there. There were other times when Joseph had been there for Porter. Porter had been kept in jail many times during those years. One time when he got out of jail Joseph built Porter his first saloon. Joseph built it on the first floor of the mansion. Emma had walked in and upon seeing the saloon informed Joseph that the saloon must go or his wife and children would not enter the building again. Joseph had the saloon removed but deeded Porter land next door for him to build another saloon. So at that time Porter started his second saloon. Porter had walked away from that business in Nauvoo just as many others had when they vacated Nauvoo because of mob pressure. When they got to winter quarters Brigham Young had asked Porter to go back to Nauvoo and help the final groups of people move out of Nauvoo. After Joseph was killed Porter shifted his dedication to Brigham and was willing to do anything asked of him. As Porter rode back to Nauvoo he thought of a way to distract the mobs to leave the last members to finish their preparation to travel.

When Joseph and Hyrum were killed in the Carthage jail, Frank Worrell had been one the guards that had stepped back and let the mob enter the jail cell to fire their weapons. Frank Worrell since that time had become a man who was very unpopular with Porter. Porter and a friend had paused on a country road when Sheriff Backenstos rode up on them. He was being pursued by a mob and deputized Porter on the spot. Sheriff Backenstos feared for his life because of his pursuers. As the mob topped the hill Porter drew a bead on the lead man and he fell from the saddle dead before he hit the ground. The rest of the mob turned and went the other way. When Porter, Sheriff Backenstos and Porter's friend investigated the body, it turned out to be Frank Worrell of the Carthage jail incident. Porter wasn't at all sad that it was his enemy, Frank Worrell.

So as Porter mulled over how to distract the towns people of Nauvoo, he decided to volunteer to be tried for the killing of Frank Worrell. When he arrived in Nauvoo, he fired his pistols and was arrested. Porter rode into town with two double barrel—sawed off shot guns tied on each side, two bowie knives, a pair of Colt revolvers, and enough spare cylinders to shoot over seventy times without reloading. Porter was eventually arrested and he spent 4 months in jail awaiting trial.

Almon Babbitt was assigned as his attorney. Interestingly Babbit had been Luanna's attorney when she had divorced him. When Sheriff Backenstos testified that Porter was acting under the authority of a deputy and he had been defending the sheriff, he was quickly acquitted and allowed to go. The proceedings had bought the remaining Mormons enough time to ready themselves and they had moved on.[2]

[2]   Porter Rockwell, Rockwell and Borrowman, p. 88-89.

PLENTY OF WORK

Ike knew he had created plenty of work for himself. He certainly was glad to hear his father act so excited about his getting started with his life. He could feel Ransom's pride when he considered his son and that was a great feeling having your father be that proud. They had Ransom's cabin to finish, the barn to finish and at least his cabin up with a roof on before the winter storms hit too hard. They started early and finished late each day, and they made good time. They finished Ransom and Rhoda's cabin and finished planting the crops. They barely got the crops in in time for the plants to get enough height to shade the ground from the heat of the summer. It was essential to get the vegetable garden fenced to keep the wandering animals out. When they finished that, the summer was almost gone and the three of them started on Ike's cabin. They were then able to spend most of the day on the cabin because most of the other work was finished for now. They knew there wouldn't be time to plant Ike's crops that year so all their time was focused on his cabin. With 12 hours a day being spent on Ike's cabin they made good time.

"Ike, you better spend a little more time with Mary or all of this will be for naught," said Ike's dad.

"If I knock off a little bit early will that be okay today. I am seeing Mary pretty soon,

"Well, if we are to have this work appreciated we better let you go," explained Ransom. "Frank and I will finish this row of logs and then we will come in also. Have fun and say hi to Mary for us. We think she is a pretty special girl."

That evening was one of the best nights Ike had spent with Mary. He loved to talk with her.

"Mary, you better stop seeing me. I'm getting pretty attached to you. You better run from me or I might ask you to marry me one of these days," said Ike.

"Hmmm. I enjoy my time with you too, Ike," said Mary.

TOUGH GUY

Ike stepped out of the dry goods store with an armload of farm tools and put them in his wagon. He walked around the horses to pat them on the necks and talk to them. He loved his horses and knew they worked hard for him and always wanted them to know he knew that.

As he got to the head of the second horse someone yelled,

"Potter, stay away from my girl or you will know the whatfor".

Ike turned around slowly but he already knew who it was. Ike had never run from a fight in his life, but he also didn't go looking for one.

Ike had only been in town for a few months and he didn't want to make any enemies. The one thing he had learned in his life was the importance of friends. Friends were forever and longer. He hoped not only to make friends here in the valley, but to get to know some Indians. While he had been living there he had been watching how the Indians were being treated. He really felt the Indians had gotten a raw deal in the West. It seemed the whites had done all possible to make their lives miserable. The whites had killed the buffalo like there was no end to them many times just for their hides. The beautiful shaggy animals that ruled the plains like waves of the sea. It was said by many a wise man that you could see a herd of buffalo, make camp, fall to sleep for the night, get up in the morning, make breakfast, and pack up to get on the trail and the buffalo would still be moving past your camp. Ike himself had ridden up on hundreds of them stripped of their hides and the meat left to rot in the hot sun. The last time Ike had set on his horses for what seemed like hours just looking at the majestic animals, stripped of their dignity, lying in the dirt, fodder for the insects and scavengers. It hurt his heart and he further felt how his red brothers must think as they too saw these sights. He knew this wasn't the only time the buffalo were left like this. Oh, if only the white man had foreseen the need to not ravage the land. Ike knew the Indians had been very good protectors of the land before the white man came. They had only taken what they needed and had always knelt by the animal after the kill to thank the animal's spirit for letting them use their bodies to feed their families and make the clothes they would need especially in the cold winters. The Indians would use all the animal parts, the stomach linings to carry water and the sinews for their bow strings. The Indian was very much at peace with the land and would never have taken more than was needed.

Ike turned and there stood Elmer, feeling tough with two of his buddies close by. Ike had noticed that Elmer never seemed quite as tough unless he was trying to impress his friends. Ike carried a gun on his hip but knew better than ever to use it unless it meant his life and last thing he wanted was trouble in this new town. He wanted nothing but to make a new start here, but Elmer wanted trouble and as long as his friends were near, Ike knew there would be trouble.

He had spent enough time with Mary that at some point he had every intention of asking her to marry him. It would take Elmer and wild horses to keep him away from her. Mary was a pretty girl and when he talked with her, it seemed they could talk about anything and be thinking the same thing. Girls like that are hard to find. As a matter of fact Ike had gotten the land from the Bishop and started a cabin for he and Mary to live in, that he thought was way past leaving Mary alone. But now, Ike had his hands full with loud, obnoxious Elmer Judd. Ike knew that men like Elmer were mostly hot air and he knew just how to handle men with large amounts of hot air. He patted his horses one more time and strode across the street toward Elmer at a fast pace. Elmer was surprised to see his quarry walking so quickly toward him. He wasn't sure of his next step. Elmer had always been able to intimidate his bullying ways with his mouth. Ike felt that if this bully wasn't dealt with now, it would be a never ending thorn in his side. Ike never said a word to Elmer he quickly walked up to him, hit him once in his stomach and as his head came down, he hit him once on the side of the face. Elmer fell in the dirt. Ike was there to make friends if it were possible, not to make enemies. Ike made some small talk with Elmer's friends to try to smooth things over before he walked away and went back to his horses. He never looked back to see how Elmer was. He had other things to tend to.

As Ike drove back to his house he had recently begun he sincerely hoped that the trouble with Elmer Judd was over but a thought continued to linger that he hadn't seen the last of trouble with Elmer. He had better things to do than worry about him, but the thought occurred to him, what if they made Elmer a bishop. Wouldn't that be a nightmare! Ike loved the church and he knew somehow that that would never happen. Ike believed the leaders of the church chose their bishops wisely and right now he thought Elmer would make a poor choice for a bishop, but crazier things had happened before.

As his work went smoothly his thoughts would drift to Mary and how much he loved talking to her. Most girls talked of silly things like how beautiful would be their wedding when they got married. They would also spend hours talking about the parties they had been to and how nice it was that Elmer had built that enormous room on his house to have parties. Ike loved to talk to friends and meet new people, but it certainly didn't fill his mind most of the time. As Ike thought of Mary he also thought if he and Mary got married that he might even marry another woman as well as Mary. But he was already had a feeling that no matter what Mary would always be his favorite. The present policy of the Mormon Church was to award more land to men who had large families, so why not marry more women. He knew of a man named Williams that was asked to move from Payson to Moroni and he began with 20 acres. He was a bachelor and each time a new family needed more land they halved his land. Finally he ended up with very little land. The church had also been known to take men's land away if they didn't properly care for their land. Ike was smart enough to read between the lines and think about marrying more girls. He wanted to have a fair portion of the land.

But often his thoughts returned to Mary. He liked that girl. Not only was she the prettiest Ford girl, but she and he could talk and talk and talk. She liked to talk about the mountains which was Ike's favorite topic. She loved the deer and elk just as Ike did. She loved to wake up in the morning on the top of a mountain with elk grazing at her feet. She liked to watch the animals as they went about what animals go about. She was his kind of girl. Ike was totally content spending time in the mountains, seeing the animals in their natural surroundings. Ike had always loved to watch deer, especially when they didn't know he was there. He could spend hours watching them browse along and see their ears pop up and their heads turn at the slightest sound. Whenever they decided to move quickly the majesty of their bounce touched every fiber of his body. They were just plain beautiful. Oh, how he loved to see the deer. Then one day he started paying more attention to elk. Deer were truly beautiful, but elk were majestic. He looked so forward to being in the mountains in the fall when the elk were bugling. Once his focus became mostly elk, many times he would ride past deer hardly noticing because elk had taken his interest. He had learned to imitate the elk bugle and many times the bulls would come to him to see is he was another bull. He and the bull would usually leave friends unless he needed the meat.

Even though Ike loved to be in the mountains he also loved to work. He liked the feel of tools in his hands and seeing things get done. He liked how it felt to fall to sleep after a hard days work. He never slept better than when it had been a busy day. Ike had come west with his father Ransom and they now had become fast friends. When he was a boy many times they hadn't agreed, but Ike had learned that it was best to listen to his father, because even though at the time Ike was sure he was right and his dad was wrong, later he would realize that his dad's ways were the best and he respected his father. As this respect grew they became good friends and he knew his dad would always take the time to be there for him.

Ransom had learned to respect Ike as well. But Ransom was a little worried about Ike and Mary. Ransom had heard of Elmer's desire to marry Mary. Elmer was already married to two of Mary's sisters, and Ransom couldn't help but think that it spelled trouble. Even though he and Ike had a great relationship he knew that when it came to some things he needed to leave it alone and Ike's love was one of those things.

Saturday night there was a dance in Elmer Judd's big room and Ike wanted to take Mary to that dance, but he was wondering if that was a good choice. After the earlier problem with Elmer that week that might fuel that fire with Elmer. He thought about it and decided he wasn't about to let Elmer run his life. After his work was finished that day and he spent a little time working on his cabin he was thinking of trying to talk to Mary about the dance. He would never knock on a girl's door after 10 pm. That to him wasn't the right thing to do. It wasn't 10 yet so he rode across town, tied his horse to the hitching rail and stepped to her door. Mary's father had died recently and Elmer Judd had already married two of Mary's sisters. That thought continued to bother Ike. He knew that was part of the reason why Elmer thought he should have Mary. She was the prettiest of the three.

As she opened the door he thought, "Truly she is the prettiest of the three and more than her looks she had a wealth of sense and good sense was what he was all about." Mary's mother was okay with her talking and once again she proved to him why he liked her so much. All of the things that she talked about were just what Ike liked to talk about. The mountains, the animals, a horseback ride, and they even agreed about the plight of the red man. Oh how he liked that girl.

She agreed on the dance Saturday and just as helpful she was fully aware that Elmer could be a problem. Saturday night arrived. Ike couldn't get there as early as he had wanted. Taking good care of his animals was a priority to him. Once they were curried and grained he hurried over. Mary, as usual, was in great spirits. Even though she had lost her father recently, she had the pioneer spirit that was about moving on and letting the past be the past. There were times when Ike could tell she needed time to grieve, but she was good at thinking of the future. The dance went well and they enjoyed their time together. Elmer only tried to cut in once and Mary told him that she was with Ike and she wanted it that way and nothing else was said. Ike hoped that would be the end of any problems with Elmer, but he thought he doubted if he could be so lucky.

THE INDIAN

Ike had had little time that summer to go up into the mountains, but one Sunday he had rode up Spanish Fork canyon. It was a beautiful summer day. It was still cool in the morning and he loved the feel of the cool air on his face. As he rode he had seen little wildlife that day, but it still was invigorating and something he loved to do. He touched his horse into a little run and he came around a bend in the trail and there was an Indian. He had to rein in quickly to avoid hitting him. He spun his horse around to look at him squarely. The Indian was carrying arrows on his back and a bow in his hand. Ike had no idea what to expect. Would this be an ugly encounter or a friendly one? Only time would tell that one. Ike broke into a big grin and the Indian smiled back. Somehow Ike knew this Indian and he would become friends. Ike thought, how does a guy know that that soon. He remembered hearing Brigham say that the Holy Ghost tells us things if we but listen. Maybe that was a prompting from the Holy Ghost. He wasn't sure. But that grin he got back was worth a whole sack of gold, of course Ike had never seen a sack of gold, but he thought it had to have been worth it.

Ike so wanted to be able to talk to this Indian in his own language. He knew no Ute words at all. Ike thought, where there is a will there is a way. He tried his hardest to communicate with this Indian and accomplished little. He was able to communicate a little with hand signs and he was glad of that. The Indian seemed more comfortable after a time and wanted to continue to talk more with this white man. After some time the Indian motioned for him to follow him. They rode along silently for some time. Ike then found himself on the edge of an Indian camp. He was surprised. He had felt the Indian had trusted him but not that much. Of course this could end badly also. His companion rode into the center of the camp and motioned for him to follow. An Indian came out of his lodge and signaled to sit down and talk. Ike thought, this will be fun. How are we going to talk? I don't know their language. To his surprise the other Indian knew his language. He said his name was Antonga, but the whites called him Blackhawk. The conversation went very well and as they talked Blackhawk helped him learn some of the Ute language. He told him that the first Indian's name was Mountain. He could feel a trust developing in just a short time. As he rode away he thought he had found some new friends and he was excited about it. He wondered how Mary would feel about his new found friends. He also wondered how Ransom would feel about his new friends.

When he got back into town he rode straight to his Dad's cabin.

"Dad, I've some interesting news," said Ike. "I've not too sure how you will feel about it. You may be upset with me.

You may judge me. You may think I am a fool. Of course, the only part of me that is a fool is your part. Mom's part is just good common sense, not nonsense."

"What in the world are you talking about? Sometimes you remind me of your mother. Talk and talk and talk and never really say a thing," said Ransom.

"Dad, you know you are walking on thin ice. Look, behind you," laughed Ike.

Ransom spun around to see his wife standing there.

"Your Dad is on such thin ice that the ice has already melted," said Rhoda. "He thought he might be invited to Sunday dinner, but now he is uninvited."

"How can the guy who provided the meal be uninvited," murmured Ransom. "Without me there would be no meal."

"No, without me there would be no meal. Would you like to see how fast that meal can go in the dirt?" said Ike's mom.

"Okay, okay, you are so right. I humbly apologize. Would you please forgive me for all my mistakes in our lives?" laughed Ransom.

"Ha, that will be a lifetime endeavor. Let's wait and see if I have that much forgiveness in me. I doubt it. That is a lot of forgiving," commented Rhoda.

"Oh, by the way, Ike did you have something to tell us, when your mom so rudely butted into our conversation," said Ransom.

Rhoda growled and said, "Ike, I apologize for your father. He has no manners…."

"Wow, now I see how you make a marriage work. Sometimes I worry about that. Even the great Porter Rockwell was divorced by his wife", commented Ike.

"Of course you know your Dad and I are just kidding, don't you?" said Rhoda.

"How long have I lived with you? I guess I know about all there is too know about you two," said Ike.

"Well Ike, let's not go there. You know a lot about us, but not all there is to know," commented Ransom. "Now, you were excited to say….?"

"Well, this morning, early I rode up Spanish Fork canyon and it was a beautiful ride. The air was so cool that you could taste it. It was beautiful. It couldn't have been any more beautiful."

There was a long pause and then Ransom said. "That is what you wanted to tell us. You made me stand here all this time and that is what I waited for?" growled his Dad.

"Well, not exactly, I was riding along and enjoying the ride and then……" said Ike.

"Yes, yes, you told us that, "whined Ransom.

"Then I rounded this corner and who did I run into and almost hit him and his horse?" said Ike.

"I suppose it would have been well if it had been Elmer Judd," commented his Dad.

"Well, I wasn't that lucky. If it had been Elmer I may have enjoyed running over him, that guy…." Ike said. "No, it wasn't him, it was an Indian."

Rhoda said with a worried look on her face, "We haven't heard of any trouble with the Indians. They are peaceable and we see them fairly often. Was it a problem?"

"Actually it worked out very well. The Indian and I talked for a while, well, as much as you could call our communication talking. We were doing mostly sign language, then he took me to his camp and I met THE Blackhawk and he speaks English. I actually had a great time and I think I have made some new friends. I felt like I could really trust them. The first Indian's name was Mountain. You know sometimes you can feel if you can trust someone and I felt that they were the kind of people that if they said they would do something, they would make it happen if the good Lord was willing and the creek didn't rise. I am so glad I was lucky enough to meet Mountain on the trail. I have wanted to meet them since we got here," commented Ike.

"I hope you don't live to regret that meeting," thought Rhoda out loud.

"Why could their meeting possibly affect Ike or us," said Ransom.

"I can think of about a thousand reasons. How many Indians are close to this valley? Yep, about a thousand, and there will be trouble in the future. The whites have killed off most of the buffalo, the deer and the elk, many times on purpose to make the Indians starve. How can there not be trouble? All these delicious looking cows here in the valley with winter coming on, at some point it will have to go badly. All it will take is one stolen cow and this entire country will erupt. Brigham says we ought to feed them, not fight them.

That will work fine as long as they steal someones else's cows. I can name ten men that just will not tolerate a cattle thief," commented Rhoda. "Will you, Ransom, let them take your cattle. We have so few anyway."

"Sometimes I wonder why I married this woman and then at times like this there is not a shadow of doubt why I married her. Look how insightful she is. She is probably the smartest woman in the entire valley, maybe the entire world. I am one lucky man to have her under my roof sealed to no other man than me. How could a man be so lucky?" said Ransom.

"Times like these you earn a few brownie points, but you need about one million," laughed Rhoda.

"Your mom has a point. Now we see Indians fairly often and they seem peaceable enough, but wow, if there ever is real trouble maybe all of the Indian tribes that are close or not close will unite to avenge who knows what," commented Ransom. "It is a powder keg ready to explode. If the whites would stop their killing of their food supply, there may be trouble avoided. Given a few years now the herds could build back up to an amount to save the Indians food. There is a town meeting coming up. I will try to talk someone in to going to Brigham Young and stop this before it is too late. I have a feeling that even if Brigham sent out an order to stop the killing, it would make no difference. The people do listen to him but there are a lot of head strong men who would continue to kill the animals. How would you control something like that? So many are convinced that there isn't room enough for the Indian and the white man to both live here and do fine together. I think we could work together and turn this into a great place to live. We can let the Indian and the white man live side by side. Many of them could be converted and live just like we live, given time and some brotherly love which I believe is what we are supposed to be all about. Didn't I read that the second greatest commandment is to love your brother as yourself and laughed Ransom, I certainly love myself?"

EMILY

P orter rose early one morning. He saddled his horse and went up into the mountains. He never grew tired of his rides in the mountains. As he rode he thought of Emily. He had been so proud of her and glad to see her when she had come out with that handcart company. She had come most of the way entirely by herself. He thought most of the way by herself, but he knew there had to have been some help along the way and he felt like any help she had received had been very much appreciated. He thought it had to have been impossible for a 15 year old girl not to have been given a little help.

Porter had been so glad to see her. He had written many letters and the last one he had received said she was coming because her stepfather had been too much for her to handle. Later on when they talked she indicated that Alpheas Cutler was being a good father to the other kids. Porter had sorely missed his other three children and was so torn by where he needed to be, here or there to be with them. Emily had also brought the news that Luana had been pregnant when she had left him and he had another son he hadn't known about. He had been named Jacob and Luana intended that

Jacob would never know the name of his real father. That hurt him as well. He had two sons somewhere in Minnesota and here he was hundreds of miles away. Alpheas had started his own church and then Luana had taken up with one of his flock and they had moved to Minnesota. That woman never ceased to get his goat. He had had some to say about Luana in front of Emily but that hadn't gone well. Emily felt that she loved her no matter what and she loved her mom. He had had to leave that subject alone not to hurt Emily and he certainly hadn't wanted to do that. Emily had been through a lot and didn't need his scorn on top of everything else. Porter had learned to be quiet about her mom and so had Sarah his mother, but Sarah's other children weren't nearly as careful. They had made it clear of their disrespect for Luana. Once Emily had known their sentiments she had stayed away from them. It had even hurt her time with Sarah, her grandmother. Porter's siblings were usually around Sarah and so Emily just stayed away. She couldn't bear to hear her mother criticized. That had made her time here a little tense and lonely. It may even have affected what had happened next.

Some of Lilburn Boggs's cohorts had kidnapped Emily and taken her to Sacramento, CA. That had nearly broken Porter's heart. He was so worried about her and never rested until he found her in the gold fields of California. By that time she was married to one of her captors and that had nearly broke Porter in two. He had totally disapproved of her marriage to Hiram Gates. He hadn't approved of Hiram's family or the way he conducted himself. He had been sick about all of it. Emily had convinced Porter that that was what she wanted and who was he to decide her future. He suspected that part of it was no one would probably have been good enough for his daughter. It is a problem shared by most fathers.

Now here he was on top of a mountain admiring one of the prettiest sights in America feeling alone with his children spread out all over this country. At least now maybe he could rest a little being half way between Emily in California and the other four the other direction in Minnesota. Besides his place was here helping Brigham with this new adventure and it had been an adventure. Brigham had recently made him a deputy marshal so he had his job to do. There had been some outlaw types that had recently moved into the area and Brigham had felt that they needed to be watched. He thought sarcastically that when Emily's clan found their way back up here they might be the worst of the lot.

BLACKHAWK AND
MOUNTAIN

Whenever Ike had time, he rode up into the Sanpete Valley to spend time with his new friends. Time was not something he had a lot of, but sometimes friends need time also. If there was anything that Ike had come to know was the value of friends. One thing Ike liked to do was hunt with Mountain if there was time. He knew he had to be there very early to make that happen. Mountain always liked to be in the best place at first light. Ike had come to know some Ute language. Blackhawk had been quite helpful because he had lived with the whites for a time. After Blackhawk's family was killed the Mormons took him in in Salt Lake. He lived with them, ate with them and went to church with them. Whenever the Mormons got a chance they tried to convert the Indians. They believed the Indians were the last remaining people from the group of Israelites that left Israel in about 600 B. C. and they wanted to convert them at every turn.

Ike's father had taught him a great deal about hunting when he was a boy, but he found Mountain was the best hunter he had ever met. He knew how to build snares and traps to catch any animal. He knew the very best time to be there and the best place where they might be found. He could tell you how long ago an animal had passed that way within minutes. He had a sixth sense about where the animal would go from there and many times they would arrive before the animal did. Mountain, whenever they were successful, would kneel beside the fallen animal and thank the animal's spirit for the use of his body. It fascinated Ike to listen to his prayer. It was not a lot unlike the prayers he had heard all of his life. Mountain then would find a use for almost all of the animal's parts. It amazed Ike how unwasteful he was. Ike would often think there was so much whites's could learn from the Indians if they would but listen. The one thing that especially impressed Ike about all the Indians was if they said they were going to do something, it would happen. You could always depend on an Indian's word. He thought about how many times he had agreed with a white friend to meet to go do something as a boy or even now as a man and the white wouldn't show up and wouldn't even bother to let him know in advance. Sometimes he wouldn't even know what happened until days later when he ran into the friend.

Ike very much enjoyed his association with his new friends even though his mom and dad were a little concerned about it. Ike came in just about last light one evening and he saw his father out in the yard.

"Son, are you sure your spending time with your Indian friends is a good idea. Of course you heard about the Utes that attacked that surveyor crew down south not very long ago, "said his father.

About that time his mom opened the door.

"Hey you guys, come in the house. It is getting chilly out there. What were you talking about anyway?" commented his mom.

"See I told you that nothing goes on around here that your mom doesn't get involved in. Did you invite her to stick her nose in our business," said Ransom.

"Now settle down you silly men. I work around this house all day and when I get a chance I like to talk to someone, I take every opportunity," blustered his mom.

"I guess you do have a right to know what we were talking about. Even if you didn't have a right you would find a right, right mom," laughed Ransom. "See, son this is how a marriage works, You have a little fun, but you make sure no one's feelings are hurt. Mom, have I ever really hurt your feelings?"

"No, I always know when you are serious. We wouldn't want our lives to get too boring. If it was too boring I would have to find another to make my life more interesting." laughed Rhoda.

"Now, don't get any funny ideas or I will sell you to the first gypsy group that comes through, cheap. I might have to pay them to take you, "smiled Ransom. "I was telling Ike that maybe his spending time with the Utes wasn't such a good idea. Folks are still pretty upset about those Utes killing that surveyor crew down south. I don't think it was Blackhawk's band, but who knows. Captain Gunnison and 7 others were killed and it wasn't too pretty of a sight. When folks start finding out how much time you are with them, you might even get blamed for it. There were some rumors that it was

actually some white men dressed up as Indians. Some folks
don't want the railroad and telegraph lines coming through
that part of Utah."

"When the day comes when others can pick my friends
I won't be very happy. I've found in many ways they make
better friends than some white folks. When an Indian tells
you something is true, you can depend on it being true,"
commented Ike.

"Let's back up and take a careful look at what is going on.
I read this in the paper yesterday and it really made me think
about how non-Mormons feel. It came out not too long after
Joseph Smith was murdered, but it still makes you realize
how non-Mormons feel," said Rhoda.

"The great aim of Joseph Smith was evidently to cloth
himself with the most unlimited power, civil, military and
ecclesiastical, over all who became members of his society.…
He stated that Emma his wife, was of Indian descent, in a
line from one of the tribes of Israel. That he (Joseph) was a
descendant from Joseph of old through the blood of Ephraim.
And that God had appointed and ordained that he, with his
descendants, would rule over all Israel, meaning the Latter Day
Saints or the Mormons, the Indian tribes and ultimately the
Jews and Gentiles.…Joe further stated, that God had revealed
to him, that the Indians and Latter Day Saints, under Joe as
their King and Ruler, were to conquer the Gentiles and that
their subjection to this authority was to be obtained by the
sword! From this revelation…Joe was accordingly crowned
KING under "God, over the immediate house of Israel.…It

is also a fact, ascertained beyond controversy, that the Indian tribes of Sacs and Foxes, Siouxs and Potowattamies, were consulted, and their assent obtained previous to the mock crowning of this unmitigated Impostor, and that delegations were sent to Nauvoo from each of the above tribes about the time of the coronation ceremony…These delegations of Indians were seen by hundreds and hundreds at Nauvoo, (the Mormon capital in Illinois).[3]

"Wow, I would like to think sentiments like that were long since forgotten. We do believe the Indians are descendants of the Israelites, but all that other stuff is nonsense," commented Ransom. "I wish the world knew what a great man Joseph was. They have totally missed his essence. We were so lucky to have had him in this time and we lost him because of narrow minded people."

"I think what your dad is trying to say is be careful and make sure what you are doing is what you totally believe is the right thing and that you will exercise thought at all times. Sometimes folks jump to conclusions and think the wrong thing. They let their own feelings get in the way of reason. Seeing you with the Indians when people are getting killed is tough for folks who know people who have been killed and that is hard to swallow," said Rhoda. "Be careful and keep in mind the consequences of where you are and who you are with."

---

[3]   quoted In Hallwas and Launiul, Cultures in Conflict, p. 103-107. George T.M. Davis, as

"Thanks mom, I will give it some thought, but when you have found friends who you believe probably have a greater right to this land it is hard to turn your back on them. Do you understand how I feel, mom?" explained Ike.

"I understand exactly what you are saying, but what I said still holds, be careful and think of the consequences. It might be disastrous," said Rhoda.

THE HOMECOMING

P orter had been very torn by his not being able to bring Emily back home. He had stayed for some time in California. While there he had run into Agnus Smith, one of Joseph Smith's sister in laws. He was so glad to see her, but amazed when he found she had no hair. Agnus told Porter she had lost her hair due to Typhoid Fever. Porter had felt a real need to be there for her if there were some way possible. After much contemplation he decided to have his own hair cut off to give his hair to Agnus in a wig. Agnus was so touched she cried when Porter presented her with his gift.

After Porter had given his hair away he felt that he had broken an agreement to both Joseph and God. He had been promised he could never be killed as long as he didn't cut his hair. He was in anguish for having fallen short of his promise. He also felt vulnerable in a new way he wasn't used to. He spent some time by himself not very eager to rejoin society and the possibility of some altercation. Porter was quite glad as his hair grew longer. Porter in his anguish over both Emily and his hair started drinking heavily while in California. One day while laying drunk he felt he had a sign from God to start a business while in California. He decided to call it the Round Tent Saloon. He had it up and open in very little time after another saloon had burned down in a small town. The local miners were so impressed with his efforts that he was complimented many times for his accomplishment. Throughout this entire time his dog that he called Ugly had stayed with him. He was glad for the company of this long time friend.

While in California he often thought of Emily and wondered how she was doing. He was hoped she truly was happy as she thought she could be. He couldn't see how she could be. He hadn't approved of her choice of husbands or his family, but he had found that father's don't have very much say so when their children choose mates. The thought that she had married her kidnapper had hurt him to the bone. At least she could have given him time to prove himself, worthless or otherwise. And if he was worthless maybe Emily could help him to understand the value of a good life. Porter rather doubted it. His experience told him that men unless raised to value the good things of life never learned it even if they did marry a good woman. Usually their wives suffered for their poor choices.

Porter had run into Lilburn Boggs, ex-governor of Missouri, while in California. He had walked into a saloon and there said Boggs with some of his Missourian friends. He had approached Boggs and had been recognized as he walked over. The place became quiet and all wondered what was to happen. Boggs was able to prove he still had a way with words. He outfoxed Porter somewhat and left Porter wondering about the meeting for some time. He had not accepted the accusation that he had had something to do with Emily's kidnapping but he admitted he did know about it. This to Porter was confirmation that he had in some way caused the kidnapping. As he left he often wondered if this was the last of he and Boggs or if some day they would end all of their problems. He deeply resented Boggs for all the suffering he had caused his people and his father. His father had died of exposure that winter when they were forced out of Missouri. He felt some time they would have to settle their differences, but had no idea where and when.

Porter had returned to Utah to his cabin on the north end of the Salt Lake valley. He felt the loneliness as he had never before. He busied himself with the chores of a ranch and one night as he said on the porch he saw a lone rider approaching and wondered who it might be. As the rider rode closer he realized it was Emily. Wow, he was so filled with every emotion possible, missing her but also feeling deserted for a family of rabble. His feelings were mixed and as she stepped up on the porch he couldn't look at her. He was overcome with feelings.

"Daddy, it is so good to see you. I know I have hurt you and I feel badly about that, but I hope you can understand. I had to follow my heart. I thought I had found what I had always wanted and in many ways I had. I wanted someone to need me and someone who accepted me for me and not judge me for the things my mother has done. I was truly happy and I wanted it to last forever, but it didn't," said Emily. "I'm here to stay if you will let me. There is nothing there for me any longer. I missed you Daddy, oh how I missed you."

Porter was quiet for some time and finally said, "I missed you too," as he hugged her. "Of course you can stay. You are always welcome."

Emily had told him of her experiences. Hiram had died of a fever and his two sons had been killed by Indians. Emily had lived a lifetime in two short years. Emily had asked to stay and finally Porter softened and hugged her as he never had before. He was so glad to have her back in the Salt Lake valley. There was nothing he could have wanted more. His days of loneliness were over at least for a while. Who knew what was next… So much had happened.

TIME WITH MARY

I ke was feeling strongly that he was right about spending time with his new friends. He couldn't wait to talk to Mary about it. He had arranged with Mary to see her that afternoon. It was Sunday which was about the only day that he had time for visiting.

"Hi sweet lady. I guess I need to be a little more forthright with my feelings. I think you have figured out that I think you and I belong together. My feelings for you are getting stronger every day. I just worry that someday you will become tired of me and want someone else. Divorce happens you know. I guess it is a bit of a gamble," said Ike.

"My feelings for you are getting stronger every day also Ike. I think you have to take a hard look at the person's family and what they are all about. My father has passed away and I miss him dearly. I think also that I am a lot about what my parents were. They would never have divorced if my father hadn't died. It makes my heart very happy to know they can be together again after this life. I think also how the person is raised has a lot to do with what the person can endure. I plan to never spoil my children because I think if you spoil a child they expect perfection in life and that is just not possible.

Life can be tough and you need the character toughness to make it through those times," said Mary.

"Even the great Porter Rockwell is divorced and from what I have read he was very much in love with Luana. They had built a life together and then one day it was over. The last thing I heard was she had married a man who had started his own church and then she had run off with a member of this new church and left her second husband. How can a guy depend on a marriage working? It sounds like marriage is a crap shoot. Who knows what might happen," commented Ike. "I've heard stories of how hard Porter had worked to win her heart. They were married during all of the trouble with the Missourians. They weathered the mobs tearing the roof off their house. They were together when some of the church members were tarred and feathered. How can you weather all of that and still have the marriage fall apart? I understand he and Luana had four children together and Porter recently found out that she had been pregnant when she left him and that makes five. Number five is a son that Porter has never seen. Did you know his oldest daughter has come out here to live close to her father? How hard is that for all those children? I know I am much more who I am because my parents are together and always have been."

"Haven't you just explained most of it," said Mary. "It sounds to me like Luana was probably raised to think life would be easy and full of milk and honey. There is milk and honey out there, but you have to earn the right to enjoy it and that doesn't come from giving up. Like you said, the children suffer from divorce and maybe the family and future generations will never recover from one person raised in a spoiled way. Haven't we read that mistakes in raising children will be visited on the heads of the parents for three or four generations? Wouldn't that be the saddest thing to have passed on and know the mistakes you have made and have to watch further mistakes being made because of the dumb choices you made. Wow, that would be the hardest thing imaginable for me. I can't even think about that with it not breaking my heart."

"Wow, to think of that, watching your children and grandchildren and maybe more generations not have the tools to make good choices and you not being able to do anything except sit back and watch it happen. Maybe I will never die because I don't want a ring side seat to watch my mistakes being done again and again by my future generations. It does make you feel a tremendous responsibility to do the right thing," mentioned Ike. "That is one of the reasons that I think so much of you. I think you are one of the smartest girls I have ever met. I used to think my mom was the smartest, but I think you have her beat and by the way you can't ever say that to my mom. She thinks she has the number one spot. This is just between you and me, okay."

"That is one of the reasons I like you so much is because you are able to recognize greatness all by yourself," said Mary.

"I came here to ask your opinion about my spending time with my Indian friends," said Ike. "Mom and dad are little concerned about it and I don't want to do anything different than I am doing."

"I can totally understand why your parents are concerned. There has been trouble with the Indians. Of course you have heard about Captain Gunnison and his men getting killed down south of Manti and other scraps with Indians. I just wish more people would think like you do and these troubles could be resolved. I think a greater understanding of the Indians and what their needs are is the key to all of the problems. Why can't we see that this was really their land and we just moved in and said to the Indians you have to get out of our way. Well, if someone said that to me, I would fight too. Why can't we see there is a solution? A solution can't be all that tough to figure out and I certainly don't think that lying and not even planning to keep our promises to the Indians is the solution. So far I don't believe we have kept one promise we have made to the Indians. Wow, how can we be so dumb and a Christian people to lie and try to deceive them. So why do the Indians get upset and fight back. Gee, I think a three year old child can figure that out," said Mary.

"I totally agree, I really feel if all us in the valley spent more time with the Indians understanding what they are all about and learning the wealth of knowledge they have, that the differences will just go away. They are not the savages that most whites think they are. Sure, they act different and think differently than we do, but they have been here for generations. Of course they are different," commented Ike. "It sounds like we are thinking the same thing."

"Conversations like this make me feel closer to you, Ike. Maybe we ought to stop talking to each other," said Mary.

"Sure, like that is going to happen. I think we are destined to spend a lot of time together. I don't think you can fight destiny," laughed Ike.

"You know your mom is a smart lady. You need to think about what is the smartest thing to do. There is a lot of resentment growing about the Indians and who spends time with them. You do want to make sure that the results of your being with the Indians is something you want to live with. There may be consequences for your choices," encouraged Mary.

"I know, but we have to think of others, this entire valley. The right thing to do here is get to know the Indian and find out what their needs are and help them to meet their needs. Each of us has needs. The white has the need to raise crops, feed their families and keep them warm in the winter. The Indian has the need to provide for their families as well and they have done that by hunting for generations. Why can't we all meet everyone's needs? For me it is simple and we can all live in peace. One thing that has to stop is the useless slaughter of buffalo, deer and elk. Killing buffalo for their hides is ridiculous. That is not a need. It is a whim. Killing the food supply of the Indians is also ridiculous, the deer, the elk and the buffalo. What are the whites doing? Using their heads is certainly not what they are doing. This senseless slaughter has got to stop. So I think you can see, that to stop spending time with the Indians is not on my agenda. I have to see if we can meet in the middle and solve these problems," returned Ike.

"Ike, I believe in you and I support what you are doing. I have always thought that these problems can be resolved. I support you one hundred percent. I worry though that not too many whites are going to agree with us and that may develop into huge problems," said Mary.

EMILY AND MARY ANN

So many things were happening in Porter's life that he certainly wasn't bored. Porter had become partners with John Neff to build a road and to move lumber from the canyon south of Mill Creek. John was a good man and it had been a pleasure to work with him. John already had a saw mill so they just needed to get lumber to the mill to be sawed. Porter had hired men to build the road out of the canyon and it had gone very successfully.

"Porter, how come do you work with your men to build the road. There are other things you could be doing while the men work on the road," said John. "I have a lot of respect for a man that works as hard as you do."

"I believe the work is going faster with me helping and I never have been one to let someone else do the harder work while I take the easier jobs. It's just not me to do that," returned Porter. "The upper part of the road is almost finished and then we will get started on the lower part of the road. The work is going well. We have run into a minimum of rocks and that has helped considerably."

About that time Mary Ann walked into the room and smiled at Porter. Mary Ann was John's daughter and she was only a little older than Emily. Porter felt a little embarrassed for having a romantic interest in Mary Ann, but he simply did. He would never have that interest, but she had shown interest in him since he had seen her at a dance recently. It wasn't only him but it was also her.

"Hi Porter, did you come over just to wish me a good morning. If that is why, thank you very much," said Mary Ann.

"Of course Mary Ann, your father and I have nothing to say about our partnership, but it is very nice to see you this morning," laughed Porter.

"So, you are really saying that you didn't come here to see me at all," countered Mary Ann.

"Well Mary Ann, I wouldn't be telling you the truth if I didn't say that it did cross my mind that I would get a chance to see you while I was here," remarked Porter.

Porter and Emily had moved close to the Neff's to make the work on the road go more smoothly and it had afforded Porter more time with Mary Ann and he had come to like her very much. It was so pleasant to spend time with a woman who was giving and congenial at every point compared to the complaining and whining of Luana's approach to life. Mary Ann was so easy to make happy and he fully appreciated that.

Porter over time became very fond of Mary Ann and approached Emily about marrying her. Much to his surprise she was very much against it. Emily had always hoped that some time in some way her mom and Porter would find a way to reunite. In Porter's mind that was impossible. He and Luana would never again be together.

"Sweetheart, I've become very fond of Mary Ann," said Porter. "I am considering asking John for her hand in marriage."

"You have got to be kidding," remarked Emily. "That girl is no older than I am. Do you really expect me to have a stepmother that is almost my age? If you do I won't stay. I will move to the ocean. I really belong there anyway."

Porter was devastated. How could his daughter who he had been so happy to have been reunited with twice leave him because of whom he chose to marry. Why does she not want me to be happy. Porter couldn't understand her thinking. Porter was beside himself trying to imagine not marrying Mary Ann, but he didn't want Emily to leave him. He was so looking forward to her settling here in the valley and marrying some nice boy.

Emily had been so upset she had packed that night and left on her pony. Porter couldn't imagine life without her.

Porter married Mary Ann and felt that he had come as close to heaven on earth as was humanly possible. She was such a joy to have her around. Everything she did was to brighten her new husband's life and Porter was grateful for her every move. Yet continually he was burdened with the need to bring Emily back. He had lost her twice before and couldn't bear to lose her again.

Porter's life became very eventful quickly. Lot Huntington, a young man barely 18, had robbed a Salt Lake business and had gone on the run. He had stopped in the gold fields in Nevada and there he found friends. Lot's parents who lived in the valley were quite distraught over

Lot's choices. Lot was a man of short stature and carried a chip on his shoulder.

"Lot, let's go to the saloon and have a few if you think you can reach the bar. The bar is kind of high," said one of his new found friends, Bill.

"There's never a bar I couldn't reach, cowboy. You got a problem with that. If you do maybe we ought to settle it right now. Here, let's talk about it. If I set up 5 bottles over on those posts what will you think if I don't miss any of them," responded Lot.

"There is no way that you will hit all 5 of those bottles even with that new colt you are carrying. That is a mighty fine gun but a gun can't make a man out of a shrimp," remarked Bill.

"Hold your horses. Don't be so quick to judge a man. Give a man a chance," chuckled Lot.

Lot drew his gun quickly and all 5 bottles were smashed one at a time. Not one shot was wasted.

"You have got to be kidding me. Wow. I've never seen a quicker draw and that was some fine shooting. I do know one man that's faster and a better shot," said Bill. "And he isn't all that far away. If you can bring back the scalp of Porter Rockwell then you will never be doubted in this camp again. That I can personally guarantee."

"I am so tired of hearing how good Porter Rockwell is. I just don't believe it. He's just got two hands like every other man I've ever seen. I'll tell you what. I'll make a little bet with you. I will go to Utah and I will whip Mr. Rockwell and then we'll see what you have to say. What do you have to say about that?" sneared Lot.

So Lot pulled out of camp and headed north.

Porter was awakened in the middle of the night with a loud knocking at his door. The Swede Larson was at the door frantic that his daughter was missing. He was certain it was some men that had passed through that day and he had seen them talking to Heather. They had left, but Larson suspected they had come back and had taken her. He had always taught his daughter not to talk to men like that, but children don't always do what they are taught. Heather was not a child. She was 15. Larson was insistent that the quicker the trail was followed the more chance she would be found. Porter found it very hard to leave his new wife, Mary Ann, but he knew that time was important.

Porter saddled his horse and rode in the direction that Larson had seen them go the first time. Porter was able to find their tracks and spurred his horse quickly along their trail. Suddenly in the early morning light a man jumped out of the shadows with his pistol drawn.

"Porter, I've finally found you and now we will find out who is the better man," said the short man.

At first, in the early morning light Porter couldn't see who the man was. Then he moved out of the shadows and he recognized him.

"Lot Huntington, your parents are worried sick about you. You have been gone for months and they haven't heard a word from you," yelled Porter.

"Never mind my parents. You have found your day of reckoning," snapped Lot. "Now from this day forward no one will dispute which of us is the better man. Grab leather."

"Lot, I would love to accept your challenge, but there are two problems. One is that you have already drawn on me. You have the drop on me. What would that prove? And second, I am very busy looking for a 15 year old kidnapped girl and I don't have time to help you figure out who is the better man," remarked Porter. "I think whatever is on your mind could be better solved if I make you my deputy and you help me find this girl. There is not a minute to spare."

"You would make me your deputy?" said the surprised Lot.

The thought came to Lot. If he returned to the mining camp having become Porter's deputy that would command their respect and more. Lot thought about it quickly and then said, "You will really make me your deputy?"

"Only if you quickly decide. I've got a girl to find and time is very important. We've got to go now," snapped Porter.

"Okay, let's go now. Do you have a deputy's badge for me?" said Lot.

"I don't have one on me. We will have to wait until we get back to town. Can you wait until then? remarked Porter.

"I guess I will have to."

Porter and Lot quickly rode off in the direction of the trail. About an hour later they saw the smoke from the campfire.

"Lot, wait here and I'll go closer to make sure it is them. I'll need you to make sure there is no one else to come and help," commented Porter. "Thanks for being here."

As Porter rode in carefully he wondered if there was a way to get Heather without having to kill them. That was something he always hoped would never have to happen, but sometimes it couldn't be avoided. It would be their choice. If they reached for their guns what other choice would he have.

Porter saw Heather tied by a rock and decided to ride in quickly. He wanted there to be no chance for Heather to get hurt. Soon as he rode in the clearing they reached for their guns which left Porter no choice. One after another they were shot, some standing, and some where they set with guns in their hands.

He rode over to Heather and said, "Are you okay? They didn't hurt you, did they?"

"No, I'm okay. They were talking of sending a ransom note to my mom and dad," cried Heather.

"Well now, they won't have to worry about what to say in that note, will they," said Porter.

As Lot and Porter delivered Heather back to anxiously waiting parents, Porter was glad he was able to be there for those who really needed him.

"Porter, I have some unfinished business and I am wanted for a robbery in Salt Lake. I better head back to the camp in Nevada," said Lot.

"So what, you are going to spend your life on the run. That doesn't sound too smart. Why don't I put you to work on my place and we will see if the judge will release you to me and you can work off what you owe. That sounds like a lot better plan. What do you think about that?" remarked Porter. "Why don't you go back to Nevada, finish your business and when you get back we will decide on an amount."

"Okay. I will see you in about a week," returned Lot.

Porter was still nagged about the need to find Emily and bring her home. It seemed like he had barely gotten her home and then she ran off again. His missed her and sorely wanted her back.

ELMER'S WARNING

Ike hitched up his team and as he did he patted his horses. He appreciated all these animals had done for him in getting his place together. They had hauled the timber it had taken to complete his cabin, the barn and the corrals. Of course his father and Frank and been tremendous help in getting those things accomplished, but he still thought the world of his horses. How would all of this have happened without their help, it wouldn't have been finished. Patting his horses and talking to them was the least he could do for them.

Ike had some supplies to pick up at the store and started down the lane. He pulled up to the store in town and tied his team to the hitching rail. He stepped down and he saw out of the corner of his eye someone walk up to him and stop.

"Potter, I thought we had the question of Mary Ford all worked out. I hear you have asked her to marry you. You know I am married to two of her sisters and it just stands to reason that I should be married to her and not you," said Elmer Judd with a sneer on his face.

"You know Elmer I have made it perfectly clear that I want you to stay out of Mary and I's business. Last time you messed with me, it got you nowhere. Will you ever learn? Why don't we keep this simple? You ask Mary what she wants to do and I promise I will back off if she chooses you. But if I'm promising you, I expect a commitment from you. If she says she doesn't want you, then you leave her alone forever," commented Ike. "Do we have a deal? I don't want this to keep coming up."

"I definitely want to talk to her and we'll see what comes of it," remarked Elmer.

Ike had no patience for Elmer. He thought him a brute and a bully. Mary, as near as Ike knew, had given Elmer no encouragement at all. Why couldn't he let it go and move on with his whatever he does. I guess he figured he needed to own Mary after he had helped her mom put in her crops last year. Wow, he had captured two of the Ford girls, shouldn't that be enough? Ike chose to not even worry about Elmer and his nonsense. For Ike it was just nonsense. If Mary had wanted him or even wanted Elmer now he would step aside. He had no desire to be tied up with a woman that wanted someone else. Again, it is all nonsense.

Ike was seeing Mary that evening and was as always looking forward to it.

"Hi, sweet lady, how is the sweetest lady I know? Did you know you are marrying Elmer Judd and not me?" cracked Ike.

"And who, pray tell, is deciding my future for me. I would like to know so I can personally thank them. That was such a nice thing that they did, I must thank them. We should never miss the nice things that are done for us and not appreciate them," said Mary.

"You sure are such a sassy little lady. Maybe that is why I love you so much. Actually I can't decide why I do love you so much. Hmmm, that is a conundrum for me. You are sassy and you are not that pretty," laughed Ike.

"You are a pain in the backside, Ike Potter," returned Mary. "I ought to dump you like yesterday's nightmare."

"You would never do that. You love me too much," laughed Ike. "Seriously, you are probably the prettiest girl I have ever seen. You know I don't think otherwise or I couldn't kid you about it."

"What do you think about our buddy Elmer Judd? He approached me today about not marrying you. Have you ever had an interest in him?" said Ike.

"Ike, I have never given Elmer the slightest idea that I had an interest in him. I think he thinks he ought to own me because of my sisters. Sometimes the best place for sisters is apart and see each other only occasionally. My sisters and I will do fine with me having little to do with Elmer. I seriously never showed Elmer any interest at all. Do you believe me? said Mary."

"Silly girl, of course I believe you, returned Ike."

"Yep, you are not only the prettiest girl I know, but you are also the smartest. Oh, Oh, I almost screwed up again. Don't you ever repeat that to my mom. I will be in hot water," smirked Ike. "So, have I formally asked you to marry me, if not, will you marry me."

"Nope, not unless you will marry Aseneth also. She is my best friend and I just can't bare to be without her," whispered Mary. "You know, you like to be up in the mountains with

Mountain and Blackhawk and I don't want to be alone. I know this is the first time I have brought it up, but that would please me a lot. What do you think?"

"Wow, that is a surprise. One more mouth to feed, that is definitely something to consider. I would have the responsibility of her also. That is not something a man should take lightly. If I marry her also, I want to take good care of her," Ike thought out loud. "Okay, if that is how it is then let's do it. I will tell my mom and dad exactly what is going on. I definitely wouldn't want them to be the last ones to know. You better fully discuss this with your mom. I better fully discuss it with Elmer also. I wouldn't want him to be the last one to know either."

ASENETH

Wow, Ike thought. So I thought about a second wife and maybe more but I'm not sure I'm ready so soon. I also can't imagine keeping two wives happy. How is that possible? Right now, I have been worrying about keeping one happy. There have been some divorces even in the Mormon religion and we are so much about families. How can I keep two wives happy? It's seems like a huge project, maybe more than I can handle. Maybe if one of them leaves me I might get over that, but how would I ever get over her taking my children away from me and reality is if Mary or Aseneth leaves me, then they will probably both go. The thought of losing my family would be more than I could bear. That would surely bring a strong man to his knees and maybe suicide. I can't imagine how difficult that would be.

"I just thought of something interesting," thought Ike out loud. "Maybe that is the trick to happiness for me. If say, I marry four wives and one of them leaves me or two then I still have two left I would never be totally devastated. I would still have some of the happiness that I have been promised if I keep the commandments. We have been told that if we keep the commandments and honor our priesthood that we will be blessed and to me being blessed is being happy. Losing my children would be something that certainly doesn't fall in my category of happiness. I've heard some of Porter Rockwell's divorce from Luana Beebe and I've also heard it was difficult for him. I've thought of trying to get to know him anyway, if that is possible. He is a busy man. Maybe I will make that my project for the near future. Maybe he can give me some insight into what not to do and what to do. I really doubt if that is an easy answer and since he wasn't successful at it, how would he know those answers?"

"Oh, the quandary's of life. I think I will sit down with my bishop and see what he has to say about these concerns I have. I'm pretty sure I could depend on his ideas over Porter's. At least he has been successful at his marriage."

"Bishop, thanks for spending a little time with me. I have a lot on my mind and I have some decisions to make in a hurry," said Ike.

"My best advice is never make any decisions in a hurry. You may make a decision that you will regret the rest of your life," returned the Bishop. "Decisions can be a slippery slope, if they are not made carefully. Now, young man, how can I help you."

"I am very much in love with Mary Ford. You and I have talked about her before. She and I discussed marriage recently and she requested that I marry her best friend Aseneth Lawrence. That is her condition of marriage," began Ike. "I had thought before and you and I discussed the possibility of marrying more than one wife. We talked about the acreage behind me if I married more than one. I feel rushed. I would like to get used to one wife before I married two women. I also think that the adjustment to two women at the same time would be very stressful. I'm not sure anyone has the answers to make women happy. That is a slippery slope in itself. I am a little bit at my wit's end. I am very ready to marry Mary. I love to be with her. We think like we are the same people. We agree on almost everything we talk about. She loves the mountains as I do. She thinks that the Indian issue is not such a tough thing to understand as I do. We both feel if we, the settlers, would respect the needs of the red man, they would respect our needs and all would be well. We just agree on everything. I love her so much."

"I have so many things on my mind for you. I think the first thought is, you may not always agree on everything with your wife. Few people do. Sometimes you just have to agree to disagree. Life also affects us as the years go by. Things like the death of a child, a bad year when there is not enough food to go around or the rigors of life. We also change as we get older and think differently. Having children changes our perspective. There are so many things happen that can change our life. Praying together is one of the best tools we have to stay close. Being there for each other no matter what happens builds a life together. I think slowing down and taking one thing at a time is the best answer. I would spend a lot of time with Mary and begin getting to know Aseneth. She seems like a very sweet girl, but living with someone is different than just seeing them on the street or at church. Get Aseneth in as many real life situations as you can to see how she handles stress and how she likes to do her share.

These are all good things to know. I'm excited for you and I will keep that acreage behind you for when you need it. Do you remember our conversation about not giving out land to men until they marry? Well, I took a chance with you and you have proved much to me. I like the way you helped your father to finish his place and then all of you got together and finished yours. Families that work together stay together. I believe that. I think you have a good start in life and I commend you for that," said the bishop. "It's good to air some things and talk about details that we may miss on our own. Feel free to talk anytime with me. That is what I am here for."

As Ike walked away that night from the Bishop's house he knew exactly what to do. It had been so helpful to hear another well grounded man's ideas about how to handle his questions. He needed to continue to see Mary and spend time getting to know Aseneth. He promised himself he wouldn't be thick headed and only see his caring for Mary, but he would be clear headed and take a hard look at Aseneth. If she was spoiled or difficult, it could be the ruination of he and Mary and he certainly wanted nothing to get in the way of him and her. She was the most special person he had ever met. He also was well aware that is they did all marry that he must develop feelings for Aseneth as well. Jealousy could and would cause so many problems. He needed to begin to foster fairness in all things that pertained to Mary and Aseneth. They would need equal time and caring. If either of them suspected favoritism the problems could be immense. He had his work cut out for him, but he was beginning to feel equal to the task.

The next day he began to spend time with the two of them and it was interesting to watch the relationship began to unravel. At first Aseneth was bashful and evasive, but fairly quickly she began to loosen up and be friendly. He could feel she knew there was a need to give all things a chance to become what they would become. She was witty and fun to be around. Much to Ike's surprise it was working out very well. Bringing a little humor into work and tasks made life and situations fun and interesting. Ike never had a problem finding humor in almost everything. He could have fun doing the ugliest of chores and they were beginning to find they had something special. Aseneth from the first knew the agreement and began to play her part in becoming part of the team.

THE HORSE FROM
MIDDLESEX

P orter had his hands full now with Indian problems. Porter didn't think like some of the men in the valley that Indians were just hostiles, not much more than animals. Porter felt like the Indian issue had a simple solution. He agreed with Brigham Young, it is better to feed them than to fight with them. By that time most of the buffalo had been shot and left to rot only for their hides, the deer and elk had been shot just to starve the Indians. Porter had a hard time with that kind of thinking. He knew there were easy solutions for all the needs of the Indian and the settlers. The Indians were short of patience with the whites. The men traveling to the gold fields shot at the Indians just for sport on their way to California. He was called out often as Marshal to deal with the problems. He was riding out one day to deal with a situation by Tooele, west of Salt Lake. As he rode he remembered a time on the way out from Winter Quarters with Brigham Young in the wagon train.

"After a particularly hard and dusty day, some of the men gathered around a fire after supper. It was announced a mock trial would be held, one of the favorite nighttime activities. Orson Pratt got things started by handing a summons to

Port, who read it out loud to the group, as follows; "To Marshal O.P. Rockwell: Sir, you are hereby commanded to bring, wherever found, the body of Stephen Markham before the Right Reverend Bishop Whipple, at his quarters, there to answer to the following charge-that of emitting in meeting on Sunday last a sound a posteriori from the seat of honor somewhat resembling the rumble of distant thunder, or the heavy discharge of artillery, thereby endangering the steadiness of the olfactory nerves of those present, as well as diverting their minds from the discourse of the speaker."

The completion of the reading was greeted with loud laughter. Upon hearing the laughter, others joined the group, eager to share the fun. Port handed the paper to a sheepish Markham, motioning for him to move front and center to answer the charges. The old scout refused, shaking his head, while those about him continued to laugh. Others urged him forward. He just shook his head. He was the only one not laughing.

"I wish you boys would forget what happened in church last week," Markham said. "It was too embarrassing to be funny. Just leave me alone."

I had something more embarrassing than that happen to me once," Port offered, loud enough for all to hear, suddenly taking the attention away from a grateful Markham. Port paused.

"Tell us about it, Port," a voice called out.

"It's too embarrassing to talk about," Port teased, his voice high with excitement.

"Tell us," another shouted. Everyone cheered.

Port had never much cared for speaking in front of groups, particularly in church or at political gatherings. But this was different. These men were his friends, eager to have their legs pulled. They were having a good time together. He was getting Markham off the hot seat. "It all started with a horse I bought down in Pennsylvania," he began. "Was raised in Middlesex, a town. His name was Sex, after the town, I suppose."

"You're joking," someone challenged.

"No," Port said. "But his name didn't get me into trouble until last year when Luana and I decided to see the judge about a divorce. We had pretty much agreed on how to divide things up, except for Sex, the horse." Some of the men were beginning to laugh. "Luana wanted to have Sex, but so did I. We agreed to let the judge decide.

"After the judge looked over the divorce papers Luana had filled out, she up and said, Porter won't give me Sex."

"The judge put on his specs and took a closer look at Luana." The men roared.

"Then the judge says, I suppose that's grounds for divorce."

"But, your honor, you don't understand, I said. I had sex before we were married. The judge said, So did I."

"About that time I heard a ruckus outside the courtroom, and what sounded like a horse galloping down the street. Thinking someone might have stolen my horse, I ran over to the window. The judge asked what I was doing. "Looking for Sex," I said. Divorce granted," said the judge."

By this time every man in the circle was roaring with laughter, some slapping their thighs, others with tears running down their cheeks, including Stephen Markham.

After a hard, dusty day on the trail, it felt good to let go and laugh unreservedly, at least until Brigham young stepped front and center. The laughter quickly subsided as he reminded the men there had been altogether too much cursing, bickering, light-mindedness and loud laughter. He reminded the men they were not any ordinary group of pioneers, but God's chosen people seeking the promised land- and they needed to act accordingly, so the spirit of the Lord could abide with them."[4]

That was one of his best memories and often he thought of it. It wasn't the kind of story he could tell women folk and he never had. There were certain things that you just didn't say in front of women.

They now had the new fangled picture machines, but Port was content with all the pictures he carried in his mind.

As he neared Tooele he thought about why there was so much Indian trouble. In the near past the Indians had literally lived among us. Many of them had been going to church with the members. Why all of this Indian trouble now. He knew a lot of the trouble was caused by the people traveling to the west. Many of them came without women and children. Women and children had a way of settling down the need of single men to cause trouble. That was part

---

[4]   Lee Nelson, Storm Testaments, Rockwell. Pp. 277-279

of what was happening and the Indians were getting hungrier than ever before. All of this was a dangerous mix. He knew he would need to handle the Indians just as white men. Even though he appreciated the needs of the Indian, he knew he would deal firmly with either, if they were guilty.

Brigham Young had sent Port most of the winter delivering blankets and cattle to the nearby tribes. His hope had been to settle down the volatile attitudes of the Indians. This time about a dozen Indians had attacked Tooele and taken a large band of horses from both the settlers and a wagon train that was present there. Port gathered up a posse of the California emigrants and some locals and headed south to find the horses and the thieves. They discovered about 30 Indians south of Tooele at a lake. There were no women or children or horses which suggested they were on a raiding party. They pushed them back toward Tooele hoping some of them would rather tell what they knew than be held prisoners. Near Tooele they spooked the posse's horses and killed the emigrant train's leader. They were only able to recapture four.

Those four led them south and then west into Skull valley, then again back to the north. When they were close to being due west of Toole Port realized the Indians had been successful in aiding the murderer of the emigrant leader to get away and now, enough time had passed that the chance of finding the horses or the murderer were gone. Porter walked up to the four Indians and shot all four.

A small boy was allowed to live which in Porter's opinion was enough to warn the others of their mistake and that the settlers would deal with future raids harshly. Porter certainly wasn't happy about what he had to do, but he felt like it was necessary to send a strong message.

Porter went back to his job of convincing the Indians with gifts that the great white father wanted to be friends with them and wished them no harm. Porter went north into Shoshone country. He was surprised with the attitudes of the Shoshones. They were surprised the white man wanted nothing in return for their gifts. He was offered many gifts in return including a young Indian maiden. He refused all gifts except for some horses he was given. After spending time with the Shoshones he headed east to talk with Jim Bridger at Fort Bridger which he had been told was trading guns and whiskey with the Indians. The Mormons had built a trading post close to the trail and Brigham Young was concerned why he traded guns to the Indians.

MARRIED

Ike and Mary were married in 1853 in Springville, Utah. They kept it a simple wedding and they were joined together as two in one ceremony. Ike's mother and father were in attendance as were Aseneth's and Mary's. Mary's sisters that were married to Elmer Judd were there, but Elmer was noticeably not in attendance. Ike had been true to his words as he had told Mary that he would be. He had caught Elmer in town a month or so ago and had informed him of their intentions. The conversation had been interesting and sadly memorable. Ike could still remember all the details.

"Elmer. If you have a minute let's talk?" yelled Ike.

"Yeh, I suppose I'm not too busy. What's on your mind," returned Elmer.

"I told you I would be sure and discuss your interest in you marrying Mary with her. And I did as I said I would," said Ike.

"And what did she say," returned Elmer.

"Well, I think you know because you talked to her also, correct. I also told you that if she were interested in you I would stand aside for her happiness. I meant every word of that. I have no interest in a woman if they want someone else. Life and eternity is too short for an unhappy situation. So where are you with this whole situation? commented Ike.

"I look at it differently. I have every right to be married to Mary Ford. I stepped in and pretty much took over her farm after Mary's father passed away. Since I am married to her two sisters, they should be together. They belong together. It would be no more bother to have them together. One more mouth to feed would be easy enough and they belong together. I told Mary that just the other day. It would be no bother to have one more mouth to feed. They belong together. I've been thinking Mary should be my wife for a long time and, she should. It just makes sense. I expressed these same sentiments to the bishop and he said it makes sense to him also," whined Elmer.

"You know, Elmer, I try real hard to never call a man a liar, but this time you are a ball-faced liar. I talked to the bishop just about the same time you did and he didn't say that to you. He knows I am planning on marrying Mary and he wouldn't tell you it made sense to him. How about doing me a favor and tell me one more time the bishop said it made sense to him for you to marry Mary. I want to be certain that is exactly what you are saying," retorted Ike.

"Well, that is what he meant even if he didn't say those exact words," said Elmer.

"Elmer, in my opinion, you are the biggest waste of time I have ever had the pleasure of knowing. You come up with the stupidest ideas I have ever heard of. I heard the rumor that you will probably become the next bishop here in

Springville and Lord help us if that happens. Mary talked to you and told you she has never indicated to you any interest whatsoever. Now, this time I want the gospel truth. Did you talk to Mary and what did she tell you?" said Ike. "Now I'm going to find out exactly what she told you, so this time no lying. You know Elmer, if you lie, there is a place for liars and it's not too nice of a place in the next world. So, this time tell me the truth. What did Mary say to you?"

"Welllll, she did say she had never led me to think she wanted me, but I know in time she would learn to love me and we would be happy. I've always thought she was the prettiest of the three sisters and I always wanted her for my own. I know those three sisters need to be together and we all would be so happy." stammered Elmer.

"Elmer, I will always remember your honesty today. Thank you for that. Mary and I are to be married soon and I hope you have it in your heart to wish us well. I will give Mary one more chance to be with you, but if she declines I hope you have the fortitude and good sense to let all of this go. Maybe we can live in comfort in the same valley," commented Ike.

"I can never let it go. I will always know Mary's place is with me and her two sisters. We could be so happy together. I just know it," whined Elmer.

"You have got to be kidding me," said Ike. "Elmer, just let it go. How Christian is that attitude? Aren't we about living and thinking like our brother Jesus Christ? Do you think Christ would go around pining for another man's wife. Let it go."

"Can't and I won't, no matter how much you have to say. You better change your mind about marrying her," said Elmer.

"I give up. Some people are just impossible and I found one here. See ya around, Elmer," said Ike, giving up on this conversation.

That had been the conversation that day and he so remembered every word of it. Wow, how can a man be so dense. He still couldn't believe it. Who would want to be with a woman who really didn't like him and in fact despised him? Life is too short for that. He had really thought if Mary wanted him, I would be sad, but in time I could get over it. Time is a healing thing. Right now he couldn't imagine being without her and in fact he was becoming quite comfortable with Aseneth. She was a very sweet girl and was quite willing to do her share and more. Ike could also tell that being with her best friend was such a gift. Of course, Mary had engineered that happening and now he could see the sense in it. They truly loved their time together. Life seemed to be as happy as it could be. Ike wondered if life would always be as sweet as it now was. One might think that it was only happy for Mary and Ike, but that wasn't so. They had prepared for this event as a team and it had become very important for all of them, not one withstanding.

Ike and Aseneth were not married until 1855. True to his word Ike married Aseneth but not as early as Mary had hoped. It gave Mary and Ike time to get to know each other. Aseneth was with Mary most of the time before they were married.

Whenever Ike had his work finished and had a little time he rode up into the Indian villages and spent time with his new friends, Mountain and Blackhawk. It was a very good feeling knowing that Mary was never alone. She always had Aseneth by her side when Ike had to be gone. To feed his family there may be many times when he would have to go find game or whatever it took.

JIM BRIDGER

Porter after leaving the Shoshones rode east toward Fort Bridger. He had promised Brigham he would try to find out if Bridger was selling whiskey and guns to the Indians. As he rode he wondered first if Bridger was selling that kind of stuff to the Indians and if he was, why. Why would anyone want to sell guns to the Indians to kill white men. As he thought he realized that the guns might be used on white men, but they were also more effective on game. Their old style of hunting with bows and arrows was harder to get the food they needed. He had noticed that there was less game than when they first come into the valley. He knew some whites purposely killed game to make it hard for the Indians to survive. Porter wasn't one to think that that was a good solution. For a people that had been here for many years didn't they have a right to the game first and foremost. Didn't they have a right to have their way of life that they had always had. He didn't go along with the attitudes of many white men that the Indians were in their way and they needed to get out of their way. Porter felt that they could all live here in peace. He knew the Indians may well be Israelites from the old country and a chosen people. Why do we abuse them like we do? It was getting so bad that the Indians were beginning to beg for food in the towns.

Porter had a tough job to do and sometimes it required him to kill men and he never liked it. Sometimes there was no other way. Porter tried very hard to never let there be anger when he had to kill men. He also tried very hard to never kill unless there was no other choice. Those who thought slow though often were the ones to die. He had to act quickly and most times there wasn't time to think about it. He had tried to train his mind that killing was the last resort, but when there was no other way he had learned to act quickly. It had saved his life many times.

He believed the Indians were much the same. He didn't think that the Indians ever killed for sport. Some of the young bucks may have, but kids were kids and they would be punished if they are caught, just as the white man. The Indians entire way of life was being taken away from them and they were a little upset by it, maybe a lot upset. Porter thought they wanted to peaceably live with the whites, but don't take away their way of life and their land and not expect some retaliation. It was getting tougher all of the time for the Indians. What does that do to a man's pride when he has to let his wife and children go beg in the towns for food? That would be a little hard to take for Porter. He could well imagine how the Indians felt.

Porter rode into Fort Bridger and found Bridger. He asked him for a word with him and Bridger was none too friendly.

"Jim, we are hearing that you are selling guns and whiskey to the Indians. Is that true?" started Porter.

"Porter, I know you, and I respect you. You have a tough job to do. You get most of the dirty work over in the valley, but I have a job to do also. I have to feed my family, just as you do. A man has to make a living, there is no other way. I'm sure you are aware that my trading with the wagon trains has been severely affected by those Mormons over on the trail that set up a store stealing my trade. What would you have me do? Starve. The Indians are none too happy with what you are doing to their game and taking their land. What would you have them do, just turn tail and run. They are proud people just as I am. You Mormons have pushed all of us into a corner. I sell to the Indians and they would rather trade with me than the Mormons' store. So I trade with them. It seems like they are about my only customers any more. Does that seem right to you?" returned Bridger. "If you have a better way, tell me and I am all ears. Is there a better way?"

As Porter rode away, he tried to think of a better way. Would he do the same thing as Bridger was doing? He couldn't say that he wouldn't. Life can be tough and men do what they have to do. Porter rode back into Ute country. He never knew when he might run into Indians, in fact, that now was his job to take gifts to the Indians and convince them that Brigham Young had only fair intentions for them.

He cleared a ridge. It had been a hard climb up with his pack mules behind. Sometimes they fought the lead rope and he knew that without them it would be a little easier. He was not a man to complain. The mules followed him even if it took a little longer than without them. He saw three riders high just above a grove of Quakies. It looked like two Indians and one white man. He was curious so he rode toward them. It took as much as a half hour. They were off a ways. He got closer and recognized Blackhawk and his brother. He wasn't sure who the white man was. As he rode up to them he remembered the son of the new settlers that he had seen in Springville a while ago. He remembered there had been something about him that impressed him then. What was it? He couldn't remember.

"Howdy, Blackhawk and Mountain. Long time, no see," said Porter. "And you, young man, I remember you living in Springville."

Blackhawk's English wasn't too bad. He had lived among the whites for a time when he was younger.

"We are good. We are looking for deer, but they are hard to find. Ike is riding with us today," returned Blackhawk.

"I have some things for your people. Could I ride along with you to your village?" said Porter.

Blackhawk and Mountain led out and Ike pulled up alongside Porter.

"I remember your name now. Your name is Ike Potter and your father Is Ransom. To be honest when I first saw you I was curious and I have wondered when I would see you again. I liked how you talked with your father. I like it when a father and son act like they should, respectful and ambitious. I saw both of those things in you," said Porter. "How well do you know Blackhawk and Mountain?"

"We ride together whenever I get a chance," returned Ike. "I thought my father had taught me a lot about the woods and hunting, but I have learned so much more from these two. They have good hearts. It is too bad more of the whites can't see what I have seen. They are good men. They would never use and abuse the land and all it has to offer as the white man does. I love it when they kill an animal and get down on their knees and thank the animal's spirit for the use of its body."

"Much of what you say, I believe to be true. I have often thought there are better ways to help and live with the red man than what we are doing. I do like Brigham's philosophy. "Feed them, rather than fight them.""

The four of them rode into the Indian camp and Porter spread out his goods for all to see.

"Many of the white men is the valley are no longer welcome in our camp," said Blackhawk. "Many of your people could never ride into our camp without a fight. Many of your people would ride into our camp looking for a fight. We no longer trust them. You two, we trust."

Porter and Ike rode back to the valley together. They came out of the mountains close to Springville.

"Porter, I recently almost looked you up to see what you thought about marriage. I married two best friends. So far it is going very good. I can't imagine it any better," started Ike.

"Wow. You like to jump into a bee's nest right off don't you," said Porter. "I liked being married, but making a woman happy is something I'm not too sure about. I dearly loved Luana, my wife, but she was never happy. I can't say never, I think she was happy for awhile, but she sure complained a lot. I think the hardest thing in the world is to have your wife walk away with your kids, especially when you have to move away and you can't see them. I think mine are in Minnesota. I have five. The last boy doesn't even know I am his father. I have never seen him. I have recently married to a very sweet girl. She is so much different than Luana. She never complains except she doesn't like me gone so much. I'm not too sure how that will end up. If she runs off because I am gone so much, I think that will be the last time I try at marriage. I almost chickened out this time."

"I think I have that mastered. The girl I wanted to marry insisted I marry her best friend so she will never be alone. So I married both and my first wife now is never alone. It

scared me, but I think it is a good thing. Someday I will know for sure," commented Ike.

"Here is where we part. Good luck with your wives. We will talk again", said Porter as he rode away.

HOME

Ike rode down his lane and was very happy to be home. Both of wives met him in the yard and expressed having missed him. He thought, wow, could this be any better. Maybe the Mormons had finally figured out the mystery of how to keep a woman happy while a man does what he has to do. He had spent time hunting with Blackhawk and Mountain, met and talked with Porter Rockwell. These are all things a man had to do, but if he had one naggy wife he probably wouldn't get to do what a man had to do, and that is spending time with his friends. That is just something a man has to do.

Seriously it was so nice to be home and tomorrow he would get back to work on the things around the place that needed to be done. In the morning Ike rode over to his mom and dad's and told them about his adventures.

"Hi mom, is dad around? How have you been? Are you guys keeping busy?" yelled Ike at his mom.

"I'm pretty sure he is over behind the barn. He had a cow over there that needs a little attention. How are you doing with your ready made family?" returned Rhoda. "I'm sure there are both pros and cons to your arrangement. My biggest concern is having two women in the same kitchen. Historically that produces problems that sometimes are insurmountable."

"I think the girls worked on that before they were even in the same kitchen. Aseneth is the boss in the kitchen and Mary Is the boss of everything else. It makes perfect sense to me. That doesn't mean that Mary doesn't help in the kitchen, she does, but Aseneth decides what is to be done and Mary helps out. Aseneth has everything placed where she wants them and decides what is to done first and how. Mary helps her out. Now when it comes to everything else it is done Mary's way. It is a very clever plan and it works," commented Ike. "See who comes out the smarter one is me. I was so smart to get two wives at almost the same time that were clever enough to make a household work and work smoothly."

"That sounds great on paper, but I think you are missing something and that is when you had your way and when there was one at first and then you brought in Aseneth later, the kitchen was not as she liked it and there could have been a war. So, you sir, are not the smartest one in the barnyard. Mary was. She orchestrated this whole thing and you know it," said Rhoda.

"But mom," said Ransom as he came around the corner. "He is the one who had Mary picked out and she is definitely the one who put the whole thing together. So, I believe, I have a pretty smart son. And since I brought the word up, you have a couple of pretty and nice wives. You are one lucky man. If you ever get tired of one of them, I can probably feed one more mouth. It wouldn't be any bother."

"It wouldn't be any bother!!!! Yes, Elmer Judd junior. You sound just like him and you keep talking that way and I will have one less mouth to feed," croaked Rhoda.

"Now mom, you know you will always be number one on my list. There is no other woman like you," squealed Ransom.

"Thank goodness," whispered Ransom to his son. "Now Rhoda, you know I am nothing without you and you are the total love of my life. Now, I might kid around, but have you seen me look or even heard me talk about another wife. No, you are all I can handle and more," laughed Ransom.

Just then Rhoda took off running after Ransom with a rolling pin.

"Help son, she is more than I can handle," yelled Ransom.

Then both of them fell to the ground laughing.

Ike thought to himself what would he ever do without them.

"I would have some peace and quiet," he whispered to himself.

They had been such an example to him all of his life. They knew how to have fun and yet do all that was necessary to get them here in this new land, build two homes with barns and corrals. They had all worked together, but it was done and done well. He was always thankful for Frank. He had made the work go much easier and faster. He hadn't seen much of Frank. He guessed he was off doing what young men do when the work is done. He was good about being there when he was needed though.

"Mom, dad, you knew I was off with Blackhawk and Mountain yesterday to hunt. It is sad how little game we found. I feel for the Indians. They find some game, but not nearly enough. I would like to knock the white men on the heads that have been killing the game just to make it hard for the Indians. It makes no sense. The Indians at some point will retaliate and then what. It's so stupid. I think the answer is so simple, but it is getting too late to be simple much longer. Making Indians change their way of life and plant the things they need is possible, but it sure goes against their nature. It is a tough thing," said Ike. "Can't someone change what is happening, Brigham Young or someone."

"It seems simple on paper to just say, change things and do the right thing. Many men are making the decisions to do what is done and they can't be watched at all times. Brigham has said, "feed the Indians rather than fight them," but how can anyone control what is going on. When a hunter is up in the timber and drops three or four bucks and leaves them lay. Who can control that?" commented Ransom. "You might think someone like Porter Rockwell could do it, but this a big country and ever several men can't be everywhere. I don't know the answer, but I do know, it isn't right what is happening. On the other side of the Uintahs, they are doing the same thing with the buffalo, just dropping them and leaving them to rot. It is so wrong."

"By the time they figure out what to do, it will be too late. I see more and more attacks by the Indians in the near future," said Rhoda. "And then who pays, the same men who are killing off the animals, probably their families will pay.

While they are off doing stupid things their families will get attacked and they will only blame the Indians when they ought to be blaming themselves. It is a sad thing, but how do you fix it."

"If I had the sayso, I would make a huge fine on anyone caught killing needlessly. It would be as big as they could earn in an entire season. It would be huge. They could deputize men all over the valley like a volunteer fire department and get this stopped," commented Ike. "By the time someone comes up with a good plan it will too late. The Indians are getting more hostile every day. I can feel it when I talk to them. It is a powder keg and it will explode. And imagine calling the Indians hostiles and I wonder why. It could be fixed. I talked to Porter Rockwell up on the mountain. He had some goods for the Indians. He spread them out and gave them to the Indians. It wasn't much but I know his intentions are good. We had a good talk on the way back and we think pretty much the same."

"I can't think of a better man to be thinking that way. Maybe we will be seeing something get done about it," mentioned Rhoda.

"I bet nothing will happen any different than is now happening. Porter is one man, he has a big job and most don't see any problem going on. They don't have enough respect for the Indians to really care. We can hope all we want, but my bet is nothing will change," returned Ransom. "To think of how we were kicked around back east and then we come out here and kick the Indians around. How can you not respect the Indians when quite possibly they are of the house of Israel, left the old country and come here. Sure they have changed a lot. They have been here for a long time and if you remember right who was left after their wars wasn't the best people, it was the other branch of them. I will be very surprised if it changes in time to save any of the good attitudes of the Indians. They are getting a worse attitude every day."

"What really irkes me is we are a Christian people, or we think we are. What is Christian about what is being done to the Indian? I can trust what an Indian tells me much more than I can trust a white man," commented Ike. "I believe they are every bit as good a people as we are."

THE TRIP SOUTH

When Porter left Ike and headed north he ran into Brigham Young and a group of 100 people and 34 wagons. Brigham Young beckoned Porter to come along and Porter told Brigham about his concerns. He hadn't been married very long, he was very concerned about his new bride and he still wanted to find Emily and bring her home.

"Brigham, I'm very concerned about Mary Ann. I've only been married a short time, but I still need to find my daughter and bring her home," started Porter.

"I totally understand why you are upset. I think first ought to come is your concern for your wife. Mary Ann needs you most. Your daughter may not want to come home. You told me she left pretty much in a huff. She wasn't willing to share a home with Mary Ann. I think your daughter needs time to decide what is important to her. Being here with you or being out on her own. I hope you aren't thinking of forcing her to come home. If you are, she will probably run away again. She has been married and has every right to choose her future," commented Brigham. "We certainly need you to be there on our trip to the south if we run into any Indian trouble. Your trips to the Indians have been helpful, but we still have raids on the settlements. We are hoping soon to have a meeting with some of the chiefs and see if we can make a peace treaty with them. We will have to offer them more beef and flour, but it is necessary.

"Well, let me go home and make sure everything is okay with Mary Ann and I will catch up with you in a few days," said Porter.

Porter rode back toward the cabin that he and Mary Ann had been living in close to Mill creek. He had become pretty much a silent partner in their enterprise in the canyon south of Mill creek. The lumber was coming out on the road he had helped to build and all was going well. There had been too much going on in the territory to be there very much.

He rode down his lane at about sundown and Mary Ann didn't come out to meet him, but he saw a light in the kitchen. He sat for an hour with Mary Ann telling all about his adventures. She seemed to enjoy his stories of the prairies. Luana never enjoyed hearing about his adventures. It was so much nicer to feel close to her in that way.

"When I rode up to Jim Bridger's trading post he was none too happy to explain his trading with the Indians. He said he had to make a living somehow and if it took selling whiskey and guns to the Indians then he saw no other way. I wondered as I rode away if he wasn't justified in doing what he was doing. I wondered if I was in the same circumstance if I wouldn't do the same thing. If my family needed what I could earn by selling to the Indians, would I do the same thing. The game is getting more and more scarce and guns are more accurate for long range shots. The Indians also want to feed their families and live as hunters as they always have. Shouldn't they have that right?" quipped Porter. "I ran into a farmer with Blackhawk and his brother. They were riding together and seemed as if they rode together often. We talked some about the plight of the Indians and we agreed on almost everything. He felt like if we worked with the Indians that all of the trouble we are having with them could be made to go away. I have to agree with him. We need to quit killing the game needlessly. The killing of the buffalo over on the other side of the Uintahs is ridiculous. I've rode into masses of dead buffalo killed only for their hides. I can't stomach that when the Indians have managed the herds for centuries. What are we doing to a way of life that has proven in time to be the best way and we come in here and think we have better ways than the Indians. It breaks my heart to think I am a part of the ending of the Indian way and we are doing that every day. I bet one day we will ask the Indians to move their tribes to a rocky no good piece of land and wonder then why they aren't happy with it. This man I met with the Indians was named Ike Potter. I noticed him and his dad awhile ago when they first moved into Springville south of Salt Lake. They impressed me with the way they did what they did. They have two nice places set up now in Springville. Their places look good. You can tell a lot about a man how he takes care of his place and how he keeps his gun clean. That might sound silly but sincerely you can tell a lot about a man how he cares for his gun. The cleaner the gun the more you can depend on that man to do what he says he will do."

"I don't want you to ever think I don't want to hear your stories. I love to hear about the things you do and where you go, but I do want you to know that I really miss you and I wish you could stay home more than you do. It gets so lonely around here when you are gone. I'm just really grateful my mom is close and we can talk, but it's not the same as having you home. Do you think you could stay at home more," said Mary Ann. "I know I knew how much you were gone before I married you, but it is still hard."

"That comes at a hard time. Brigham wants me to catch up with his wagon train going south with around 100 people. He was concerned about the Indian problems to the south and to be honest I am really concerned about Emily. She's off by herself and so many things can happen to a young girl out by herself. I think I need to get her and bring her back here," admitted Porter. "I can't imagine something happening to her when I could have prevented it. I don't think I could live with that."

"I totally understand how you feel, but I don't think right now she wants to be here. She seemed to have a huge problem with you marrying me. Don't you think she needs time to decide what she really wants. I'm not sure she would stay if she came home," added Mary Ann.

"That is almost exactly what Brigham said, but I still feel a great need to protect her from whatever might hurt her," said Porter. "I need to protect her. It is killing me to think about her out there, not knowing what is next for her.

Porter left the next morning with a heavy heart heading to the south. He hated to leave Mary Ann and he wanted to find Emily and bring her home. He headed south for awhile and then he turned west thinking about Emily. He rode for some time until he found the wagon train tracks. He knew they had left soon after Emily had left and he felt comforted in the fact that most likely Emily had teamed up with the train and was probably quite safe in their company.

At that point he turned back south and found Brigham's group in a few days. As he rode he thought about how often now he felt a desire to drink strong drink and why. He didn't want to feel that way, but every since he had cut his hair to give it to Don Carlos's wife, he wondered if in breaking the promise that Joseph had given him in that blessing that he was being punished in another way, that he would be plagued with a desire for strong drink. He wondered if he might wind up again in a gutter as he did in California that time. That was a hard time, but he would never forget it and he thought about it too much. Joseph had promised him in that blessing that as long as he kept his hair long he would never be hurt by bullets or knives.

Since he had broken that agreement, what would be the consequences? Would he be forever bothered by that need to drink. He hoped not, but the future held what the future held.

When he and Brigham got a chance they talked and he wanted Porter to take another trip with Colonel Steptoe to California. Brigham was looking for every opportunity to improve their relations with the government back in Washington.

SLEEP

S leep came slow that night to Ike. He went over and over in his mind what was going on with the Indians. How could they do to the Indians what they were doing? It was as if the Indians were a bunch of animals that had no feelings and couldn't think for themselves. Brigham had put a bounty on all the predators; wolves, coyotes, black bears, grizzly bears and foxes. He had even put a bounty on sparrows. How could they treat the first people here like animals? He even thought of how some people were paying a bounty for Indian scalps. How could we be so cruel to a people that he respected. There had to be a fairly simple solution to this problem and it was a problem. When is gets bad enough the Indians will begin attacking and the fight will get worse. Innocent people will die on both sides. Is it any worse for an Indian to die than a white man? Most thought the whites dying was unforgiveable and the Indians dying was no big deal. He could see no end to the insanity of it all. He sincerely wondered how God felt about all of this. He knew God had to let it happen. Men had their own free agency to make their own mistakes. Would he ever stop the deaths?

Ike finally fell asleep and as he slept he dreamed. He was an Indian brave in his sleep and he watched as many of his friends began to starve. He rode into the mountains to find game for all that were hungry, but he found hardly any. He used all the techniques that Mountain and Blackhawk had taught him, but it just wasn't enough. He was so glad in his dream to have a rifle that was good for long distance in case he saw some meat for his starving friends but he saw nothing. He exhausted all the places that he could think that there might be some animals, but again and again there was nothing. He hurt as he dreamed for the sadness and the loss of pride that he felt as an Indian. To let his family go beg for food in the white settlements and that was more than he could bear. The worst part of his dream was when he found the hundreds of dead buffalo that had been skinned and the meat left to rot. That hurt his heart in a way that he had never been hurt before. As he rode back to his camp he ran across some more carcasses of deer and elk that had been shot and left to rot. How could Christian men do this? He was horrified beyond belief.

He woke up about 4 in the morning dripping with sweat. He was so upset that he rose and found something to drink. He thought of the beef that he had jerked and dried for the winter. The potatoes and other vegetables that they had put in the root cellar for the winter. They had food to last all winter. He thought about what he could do for his Indian friends and what they were experiencing. He had hurt in his dream for them and the hurt now he was awake hadn't lessened any. What could he do for the Indians? If only every man in the valley could see what he was seeing, the problem could go away. Just as he, most white men looked at their store of food and were satisfied they were good for the winter, but what about the red man?

He remembered how he felt about being glad to have a rifle to use if and when he found game. The bows had been enough before the white man, but now they needed rifles to survive. He realized that at some point he would sell rifles to the Indians. They were in dire need of them and if it ended that they were used to kill white men, well so be it. The white man had killed the Indians way of life so maybe they; deserved what they got. That night he had not remorse for the white man. He was too upset about all the things that he had dreamed about and most of it was not just a dream. It was reality and the plight of the red man brought about by the callousness of the settlers. He wondered what was right in the eyes of God? It definitely was a grey area for him.

He rose in the morning feeling a little differently about the Indian problems. He knew he was only one man. How much could one man change things. He also had come out of the east and had taken the land from the Indians. He was as guilty as the next man. And these people that lived around him were his friends also. Friends were one of his most important assets and he looked so forward to riding around town and waving and talking to them. Nothing made him feel as complete as seeing and enjoying his friends. As he did his chores around his place he felt grateful to his wives for the help they offered in his absence. He thought how different his life was now with Mary and Aseneth. He didn't think it could be better than it was right now and he didn't have to worry when he was away about Mary being lonely, because Aseneth was always there. Both of them sometimes visited their families, but they were always home to take care of their chores. This new family of ours was their priority and it was delightful to be together. Never was there a harsh word among any of them. What a novel idea for Mary to insist on her best friend being part of our family. Mary certainly was the love of his life and he delighted in her company. He thought Aseneth might know that Mary was his favorite, but he had made every effort to not let Aseneth know that. He knew that could be the most damaging thing possible for her to know she was second. Her peace of mind could be forever damaged and Ike was very sensitive to that possibility. He knew how he would feel being second best. He literally worked hard at not letting her think that. He probably spent more time with Aseneth than he did with Mary. The last thing he wanted was for Aseneth to think or feel any favoritism. It was almost his biggest concern when he was at home.

But as he spent time with Aseneth to make her feel special he knew that Mary could see the light and the twinkle in his eyes when he looked at her. Mary felt special and Ike actually thought that he was pretty good at what he did. He thought he was pretty good at making them both feel special. How many men could accomplish that of making both women feel extra special. That morning as he worked around his place he was actually feeling a little cocky about having the ability to make both his wives feel special. He knew he would never lessen his pace at keeping his wives happy. Keeping women happy was something that had been his biggest concern before he married. It had been the main topic of conversation the last time he had had a conference with his bishop. Now he was feeling like he had the world by the tail with a downhill pull. He only wished his red brothers had the same confidence in their future.

WALKARA

Brigham Young wanted Porter to go with Colonel Steptoe to California. Porter was reluctant to go and leave Mary Ann again, but Colonel Steptoe had expressed his belief that no man knew more about the trails to California than Porter and how can a man turn down that kind of accolade. If Colonel Steptoe thought he was that good, than he would not give the man a chance to change his opinion of him. He bade his bride good bye and began the trek with the troops.

The trip to California was all that it was supposed to be and Porter headed back to SLC. Upon arriving in the valley he was made immediately aware that things weren't as quiet as it had been before he left. The word was Walkara had grown unhappy with the Mormons and their consuming of all that he saw. The forests that harbored his game were disappearing and there were now 10,000 Mormons in the valley that had once been his tribes. Walkara was now the main Ute chief and he wasn't happy. He couldn't understand why the Mormons would tear up Mother Earth to plant their food. There had been several raids and Walkara was not interested in working out problems with the Mormons. He headed south with

Porter, George Bean, and Amos Neff following close behind. They had tried to parlay with Walkara and he said no, he wasn't interested. They asked him to go to SLC to talk with Brigham Young and he said no, it was too late for talk. He did allow them into his lodge to talk and that was a little sigh of some softening. Beaverad, a sub chief of his, offered to go to Salt Lake to talk to Brigham and bring back any gifts that were given to him. A silence ensued and then suddenly Walkara pulled his knife and sliced the cheek of Beaverad implying that any decision was to be made by Walkara alone. Finally Walkara agreed to meet at chicken creek by Nephi, a middle of the road compromise. Brigham Young was to be in attendance but Walkara indicated there would be no easy terms to be met. Walkara had little or no interest in meeting the Mormons in the middle. He was very upset with the things that were happening in the valley.

When Porter got home after setting up the meet with Walkara it was just in time for his first child to be born. She was born March 11, 1855. When Porter saw the bloody scene he passed out. That much blood was more than he could bear. Porter stayed at home while Mary Ann recuperated. He very much enjoyed holding his new baby girl. They had named her Mary Amanda. As the date approached for the meeting with Walkara, Mary Ann was reluctant to let him go again. He told her it was his assignment and he had to be there to make sure it was safe for Brigham. She finally gave up and let him go. Porter loved being at home but he loved even more being out under the stars and feeling the breeze and the smell of the sage.

He, George Bean and Amos Neff were in the twenty fifth wagon of a train of 82 armed men, 14 women, 5 children and 34 wagons. When they approached the meeting place, Porter took the wagon of flour into the camp first. They also had brought 12 head of cattle to offer in the negotiations. Walkara came out of his lodge which was for Porter a sign that he was interested in talking. If he hadn't come out of his lodge Porter would have returned and not let Brigham come into camp. Porter tossed him a bottle of whiskey and he tipped up the bottle emptying the first half. As the talks began, Porter realized that that had been a mistake. The whiskey had made Walkara irritable and he began slurring his words. He began by arguing and not allowing the interpreter, Dimick Huntington, to speak. When Huntinton finally was able to converse with Walkara he told him that Brigham wanted to be his brother. Walkara demanded one of Brigham's wives, saying a true brother would share his wife. Brigham was very much against any such nonsense and offered one more wagon load of flour and 6 more beef cattle.

Walkara said the fighting would stop and motioned for Brigham to go into his lodge. There lie a very sick boy. Walkara asked Brigham to fix his son. Brigham and several of the men lay their hands on the boy's head and blessed him that the sickness might leave him. The next morning the boy walked out of the lodge, weak and white, but feeling much better.

"We brothers," said Walkara putting his arm around Brigham.

The next morning the wagon train went on south and Porter returned to Salt Lake to get the additional cattle and flour that had been promised.

MISSOURIAN

Porter was thinking things had settled down then and he was enjoying his family. He loved to hold his new daughter and take evening strolls with Mary Ann. He was thinking life couldn't be much better. He also was enjoying working around his place, even though he missed time on the prairie. It usually wasn't long until he would get an itch to be back under the stars at night.

Word came to Porter that there was a group of Missourians coming into the valley and there had already been a killing by a man named Silas Boyle. He had pushed a man at the Green River ferry to draw on him and he had made short work of him. He had shot him dead.

"Mary Ann, I guess I better go see what can be done about this man. It sounds like he is a gunmen and he may end up killing more men in the valley. As sheriff I better do my job," commented Porter.

"But you may be killed and I don't want our new daughter to be without her father. Besides I have grown quite fond of you and I would not want you to be killed. Why do you have to always be the one to take on every bad man? Can't a deputy or someone take care of this one? If enough men rode into their group they could disarm them and bring the man in", complained Mary Ann.

"Yes, that would work except at this point this Silas has done nothing we can arrest him for. The fight where the man was killed was a fair fight. Boyle goaded the man into drawing on him and then shot him. The law has to have a reason to arrest a man. So far we don't have a good reason. The other fight at Fort Supply didn't happen. One of the other men talked the Mormon out of the fight before it happened," returned Porter. "Before he gets out of the valley I'm sure more men will be killed and we don't want that to happen."

"I just worry so much when you have to go, there is no replacing my husband and I don't like being alone," said Mary Ann.

"If I were you, I would always lean on the blessing that Joseph gave me that I would never be harmed by a knife or a bullet. That should help you sleep at night," returned Porter.

As Porter rode off, he, as always, had a heavy heart for Mary Ann. She was so attentive and honestly listened to his adventures. He could not have found a better wife and in a way she had found him. He had a heavy heart for her, but still was very grateful for her and who she was. She was a very good woman.

Porter rode into the mouth of Immigration canyon and found the Missourians there. Silas was not at all what he had expected. He had expected a man dressed for the mountains and travel and what he found was a well dressed man in a polished carriage.

"I'm looking for Silas Boyle. Is he here?" said Porter as he rode up to the first wagon.

"You've found him and what can I do for you," returned Boyle.

"I understand you killed one of our men at the Green River crossing and tried to goad another into another murder at Fort Supply," commented Porter.

"The exchange at Green River was a fair fight and I didn't kill a man. I killed a Mormon. They are not men", smirked Boyle. "The coward at the fort didn't even stand up for his mother when I told him I enjoyed raping her at Far West. I've never met a Mormon yet who had any backbone. Are you one of those backboneless Mormons?

"All I know is you are not entering this valley," said Porter. "You can backtrack and meet the rest of your party on the Snake River. It won't be far out of your way. If you need a map I can provide you with one."

As Porter said his piece he had his hand very close to his colt. He expected anything from this man. He was far from over the abuse they had suffered in Missouri and had no intention of taking any more here.

"Silas, watch out!" someone called from one of the nearby wagons. "You're talking to Rockwell." Men were beginning to walk towards the stand-off.

"The famous Orrin Porter Rockwell," Boyle snickered. "How flattering. Brigham Young's destroying angel coming all the way up here just to meet me."

"I came up here to save your neck," Port added. "But I'm beginning to wonder if it's worth saving. Now, be a good boy and turn this buggy around."

"I said, I'm not going back," Boyle hissed.

"Then let's have at it," Port said, placing his right hand on the butt of his pistol. Boyle folded his arms, making it clear he was not about to get into a gunfight with Porter Rockwell. Port hoped the man was softening.

"According to the rules of dueling and established protocol, the man being challenged has the right to select the weapons," Boyle said. Port had no idea what he was talking about.

"Since you challenged me, sir," Boyle continued. "I choose sabers." Port almost laughed. Boyle couldn't be serious.

The Missourian was serious. He stepped out of his carriage, and walked around back, where he opened a long black box that contained two polished sabers. By this time a large group of men had gathered around, not just Missourians from the company, but also Mormons who were in the area.

Boyle tossed one of the swords to Port, who was thinking he ought to just shoot the puke and get it over with. But the idea of fighting with swords was interesting. As a boy, he and his brothers had spent countless hours fighting with stick swords. Here was a chance to test those skills. He liked the idea of beating Boyle at his own game. Besides, the blessing he had received from Joseph promised he would not be harmed by bullet, or blade.

Port felt the edge of the saber. It was sharp. He stepped out of the saddle, removed his gun belt and hung it over the saddle horn. Remembering one of the favorite stick-fighting tricks of his youth, Port removed a leather glove from his saddle bag and pulled it over his left hand. One of the Mormons led Port's horse away.

Boyle had removed his top coat, his fighting garb consisting of a white shirt and black trousers. He was not wearing a hat or gloves.

Port was wearing buckskins, shirt and leggings. His long hair was in a single braid down his back. He tossed his hat to the Mormon who was holding his horse.

Rockwell and Boyle cautiously approached each other. They were surrounded by a tight circle of men. Women and children were watching from wagon boxes. Port noticed that Boyle was holding his sword in his left hand. Port didn't know if that gave the man an advantage or not.

The two men stood facing each other in the middle of the circle, about six feet apart. Boyle brought his sword forward, pointing upward at a slant. Port's sword was pointing down at the ground in front of his boots.

"Touche'!" Boyle shouted, bending his knees as he dropped to a rooster crouch, placing his right hand on his hip. It appeared the man was trained in the art of fencing. Port was wishing he had just shot Boyle off his wagon seat.

"Touche'!," Boyle said again. Apparently he wanted Port to raise his blade to an upright position so they could tap their swords together to begin the fight.

Port had another idea. Instead of raising his blade to meet Boyle's outstretched sword, He began writing something in the dirt with the tip of the blade. While making the marks in the dirt he was looking straight ahead into Boyle's eyes.

"I have a secret message for you," Port said.

Boyle glanced down at the scratch marks in front of Port's boots. That was all the opportunity Port needed. His gloved left hand shot forward, grabbing the end of Boyle's sword. The same time, Port lunged forward within striking distance. Though his grip on the end of the sword was like a vise, his arm was loose, moving easily with Boyle's unsuccessful jerks to get the blade free.

At the same time Port raised his own sword high in the air, bringing it down at a slant with all his might. If Boyle had had his saber in his right hand, he might have been able to bring his left hand up to parry the blow. As it was, Port's blade had a clear path to the side of Boyle's thick neck, slicing through skin, flesh and bone. Boyle's head rolled onto his chest, then around to the right, like a ball on a string, held up by skin and sinew. Red blood was pulsing from the open neck, turning the white shirt crimson. Port let go of Boyle's blade as the body crumpled to the ground.

Dropping his own sword in the dust, Port turned away from the ugly corpse that had been a man just a few moments earlier. The men in the circle were silent, stunned and horrified. They had gathered for sport. Now this.

Port walked over to his horse and stepped into the saddle. "He didn't know I couldn't write," He said to the man who had been holding the horse. Port galloped back to town in search of a stiff drink of whiskey."[5]

[5]   "Storm Testament 6", Lee Nelson, pp. 372.

BLISS

As Ike worked around his place he wondered if it were possible to be any happier than he now was. Sometimes in life a guy just falls into circumstances that couldn't be any better. He hadn't orchestrated where he now was. If it hadn't been for Mary's request for him to marry both girls the same time he probably would have never thought of marrying Aseneth. Now they were married and Mary had been so smart to allow Aseneth to run the kitchen and for her to run other things, it was a pure delight to be in his house. He could take credit for what had happened, but he knew it wasn't his doing. The house ran so smoothly it was like a well oiled machine. The girls got along so well, but they never ignored him when he was at home. He always felt special. He was their husband and they both acted like that was important to them and they responded in that way. They both spoiled him when all of their chores were done, not too much. He knew that they had a lot to do and he didn't expect very much. A loving smile could touch your heart anytime and they both made time for that. Sometimes he got a back rub and always at least a pat on the arm or a squeeze. Often that was all they had time for and that was all it took to lighten everyone's load and reassure them that all was well.

When Ike had things away from the farm to do, that wasn't a problem. He would let them know when he was leaving and when he would be back and they were happy with that. It was such a blessing to have them never be alone. The fact they were best friends was a part of that. They had been friends since long before Ike was in the picture and it appeared to be a friendship that could last into the eternities. They had found their friendship on the migration from back east and it had become a bond, a good one.

Ike had been thinking he would like to go hunting and spend some time with his Indian friends. It had been a little while since he had seen them. The last time he had seen them was the day he had met Porter Rockwell. He had never really taken the time to access Porter from their conversation that day. Now as he worked outside he thought about it. He had liked how Porter had felt about the Indian situation. He had felt also there was a need to change the attitudes of the whites. He had also felt if it wasn't changed there would be more trouble. He hadn't acted like he intended to do much himself. In fact he could tell from the conversation that day that Brigham kept him as busy as he wanted to be. He was newly married and that took time and patience. He had commented that day that Ike had jumped into a …., what had he called it, a bee's nest by marrying two at a time. If only he had realized how much easier it had made everything. It was only one more mouth to feed. It was no bother. He laughed to himself as he repeated what Elmer had said one day. It hadn't struck him as putting too much value on his wives. He couldn't hardly imagine thinking of his wives as only another mouth to feed. No, as a matter of fact, he felt like they were a little piece of heaven. He wondered if heaven could indeed be as sweet as his life now was.

He hoped to run into Porter one of these days. He now had a reason to look him up and he planned to act on that. It wouldn't be today and probably not tomorrow, but soon. He had heard about the Silas Boyle incident. He wished he had been there and yet he wasn't crazy about seeing a man's head fall to the ground. Unbelieveable. He wasn't sure how he felt about that incident. He had heard that Boyle would have caused more problems in the valley and he thought from what he heard that probably would have been the case. He already killed the man at Green River and almost killed that boy at Fort Supply. He had been looking for trouble and people had never gotten over all of the mob action in Missouri. Ike wasn't sure people would ever get over that. The Mormons had been literally driven out of Missouri and Illinois and there had been killings. The killing of that Missourian had been, well Ike couldn't say it was justified, but it certainly stopped more bloodshed in the valley.

For any of us to stand back and criticize what Porter did or had done was way beyond our rights. He had a tough job to do and he pretty much did it alone. Ike had to admire a man that could do what he had to do and still take the time to talk to Ike as if he were interested in him. He believed Porter had been genuinely interested in Ike. He had implied he had noticed he and his father earlier and thought them to be good men. Ike's pride swelled just a little. Ike wasn't a prideful man, but when a man like Porter Rockwell showed interest in him said, he must be doing something right. Ike was proud of who he was and the quality of people his family were. His father and mother were good, church going, God fearing people and they were hard workers. He very much enjoyed some of the things his parents had taught him, things like hard work and being proud of what you had accomplished. He knew people liked them and their easy way of talking to people. They had many friends and you could tell they were well liked in the community.

He somehow worried way down in the pit of his stomach that some day that might all change and wondered why he would feel that way. It would never be a mistake they made. He thought his parents were perfect and how could they do anything to offend their friends. He wondered why that thought had crept up on him. That was interesting. Where had that thought come from, when all was going so well?

He knew not too many felt the same about the Indian situation and he wondered if some day he might make some choices that would affect his and his parent's standing in the community. That thought scared him just a little and he thought to himself he would be careful, because his and his parent's friends were some of the most important assets they would ever have on this earth and he wanted to do nothing to affect those relationships.

SADNESS

Sadness was to become Ike's companion for some time. Ike had spent last year in total bliss. He couldn't believe how happy that time had been. He had two wives that worked together as smoothly as was humanly possible. They loved each other and they loved him. Both Mary and Aseneth were always so happy when he came home. There never was any complaint about how long he was gone. He did the things he needed to do to feed his family and did many things that he didn't need to do, but just wanted to do. They never had a problem with that because they had each other. Both Mary and Aseneth were pregnant and Ike worried a little that their pregnancies would somehow change what they had. Whenever he felt that way he would shake it off and remind himself that nothing could change their happiness. It was too good to ever be different. The doctor said that both Mary and Aseneth would have their babies before Christmas. That would make a great Christmas for all of them. But whenever Ike thought about them having their babies something worried him. Why was he bothered by these thoughts? Ike knew that he had a right to personal revelation in matters about his family and he hoped that this wasn't some kind of revelation of things to come. In fact, whenever those thoughts arose he pushed them out of his head. Nothing could happen that would change what they had.

He had been able to spend a lot of time with his Indian friends. They hunted together and talked of the old times before the white man. He could feel the ever increasing tension toward the white man. Blackhawk and Mountain never resented anything to do with Ike. He knew he was accepted as if he wasn't a white man. Sometimes in their conversations reference was made to Ike directly and it was plain that he was considered to be one of their family. Once you are one of an Indian's family you are always one of their family unless you did something to lose that honor. Honor was very important to his Indian friends and he knew he would do nothing to lose his position of honor and he would do all he could to deserve that honor.

It was still getting a little harder each year to find food for the Indians families. When there was nothing to eat, sometimes the Indians would let their wives and children go into the villages and ask the settlers for food. That was a hard thing for them to do and the men resented the white man more for having to do that. Ike was hoping that some other way would be found before the Indians exploded with anger and attacked the settlers, but it was looking every day like there would be no other way for the Indians not to starve. There began to be attacks on the settlements to take cattle to feed their families. Whenever Ike heard of those attacks, he thought to himself, "Well, it was inevitable, no man will stand by and let his family starve and what other recourse did the Indians have." There really don't know how to farm and take food from Mother Earth in that way. Besides, why should they have to change their way of life which they had done for centuries just to make way for the white man. It was a powder keg about to explode.

Aseneth gave birth first on the 19th of November, 1855. It was a little girl and they named her Emily. Ike thought he had heard that Porter's first child was named Emily and he thought someday he and Porter will have to talk of that. Emily was a sweet little thing and she fussed very little. Ike was glad to keep the cabin nice and warm so little Emily could be comfortable. He delighted in doing things for his family. How could he be so lucky?

About three weeks later Mary said her baby was coming and Ike hurried off for the doctor. When the doctor examined her he walked away from Mary with a long face. He took Ike aside and said, "Ike, I hope everything goes okay, but at this point I am a little worried. The baby is turned the wrong way. Sometimes that is a disaster and sometimes it is not. If I can get the baby turned in time it won't make a lot of difference, but if I can't it could be real bad. I just wanted to warn you. For me, I always like to be warned of the worst possible thing. That way I can prepare myself in case I have to deal with the unexpected later."

"Well Doc, I hope it all goes well, because I am not sure I could handle anything going very awry. I love that woman so much and I couldn't bear to have anything happen to her. She is the light of my life and I need her, Doc, I just need her.

Please do all you can. Please save her at all costs. We could never make it without her," whispered Ike.

"Well, Ike you know I will do everything humanly possible. Well, I better get to it."

"Okay, Doc, what can I do to help you," said Aseneth. Rhoda came running through the door and said, "Aseneth, Anything I can do, I am here."

"Keep me in plenty of hot water and cloths and when it comes time to bear down, you can be by her and help her to concentrate on what we are doing."

Ike didn't hardly know what to do. He felt like he was a little in the way. Ike walked over to Mary and laid his hands upon her head and blessed her that all would go well if the Lord was willing. He couldn't understand why he had said that, but he knew when you put your loved ones in the hands of the Lord it had to be the Lord's choice. We never know what is best and the Lord does know. There would be a reason for whatever happened. After that blessing he felt like he had to be alone. He walked outside and knelt on the ground. He prayed the way he had never prayed before. He felt very uneasy and he had felt that way for weeks. He hoped that his feeling that way for weeks was not what he was afraid might happen. It scared him more than anything had ever scared him. He was sick with fear of losing her. He prayed over and over again that nothing would change, that Mary would be fine in the morning and that all would go well, but somehow he knew he must prepare himself for the worst. He had known that for weeks and he was sick about it. He went back in. He felt an intense urgency to stay close to her. He feared way down deep in his stomach. He prayed that somehow his fears would be wrong.

They worked all night to have the baby be born. Ike finally fell asleep in a chair. In the early hours of the morning he felt the Doctor shake him awake. The doctor led him outside. "Ike, we tried so hard. We saved the baby, but we were unable to save Mary. She died just a few minutes ago. I am so sorry."

Ike ran toward the door and went outside around the cabin. He threw up from the very bottom of his being. Never had he been so devastated in his life. He had lost his main reason for living. How could he endure without his Mary? He cried and cried. He couldn't stand to talk to anyone. Aseneth had followed him outside and they leaned on each other and cried together. He somehow knew that in some way he and Aseneth would be closer than ever before in their grief. They both had loved Mary from the depth of their souls. Aseneth had actually known her longer than Ike had. But he couldn't imagine anyone loving that lady more than he did. How would he ever survive? Rhoda came out and they all three cried together leaning on each other. Ransom stood back a little. He respected their grief and felt a little stifled as to what to do. He wanted to help, but how could he help. He wasn't real good at this kind of thing.

They buried Mary a few days later and it was the saddest day in their lives thus far. How could they go on without Mary. Mary's sisters and her Mom were there and surprise, so was Elmer. Ike stayed by the grave for hours and talked to the love of his life that was now gone. He missed her so much.

Ike sensed someone behind him and turned to find Elmer standing there.

"You know, Ike, I loved Mary as much as you did. I'm married to her sisters and we all loved her," muttered Elmer.

"Not now, Elmer, you are probably the last person on the face of the earth that I want to talk to right now, just go away."

"I have only one thing to say and then I will go."

"What pray tell could that be."

"I'm going to go down to the temple and have Mary sealed to me. I think it is the right thing to do. Her sisters need to be with her."

"Elmer, you really have the gall to talk to me about that right now. You have got to be kidding me. Mary didn't want you in this life and why would she want you in the next life. You have more mouth than you have good sense. If you don't leave now I am going to mop up 20 acres with the remains of your body. Now, get out of here. I have totally lost my patience with you."

PONY EXPRESS

In January the following month after Mary died, Porter Rockwell got very busy. Very few people had any idea of the pain Ike was going through. He had lost the love of his life. Aseneth was there for Ike. She had no idea how deeply he hurt, but she was hurting too. Together they grieved her passing. Ike's mom and dad were very sympathetic, but no one really knows the pain until they are involved in it. He couldn't really share the depth of his pain with Aseneth. He could never tell her how intense his love for Mary was. He wanted in no way to hurt the relationship that he and Aseneth had. They had years ahead together and he hoped in time he could become as fond of her as he had of Mary, but he knew no one would ever really replace Mary. It just couldn't ever happen.

Another problem arose as Ike and Aseneth grieved. They had a new baby to take care of. Aseneth nursed the baby but her heart was never in it. Ike felt similarly. Neither of them blamed the baby for Mary's death, but that lingering feeling that he had played his part in it still hung around. They named the baby Issac Jr. and they loved him, but when Rhoda asked after he was weaned to take care of the baby, both Ike and Aseneth thought that might be a good idea.

But as Ike grieved Porter was beginning on another chapter of his life. 'Brigham Young asked Port to speak to the territorial legislature in Fillmore. Young wanted to bid for the U.S. Mail contract between the Missouri River and San Francisco. Magraw and Hockaday, the gentile firm that presently had the contract, was averaging 40 days to carry the mail from Council Bluffs to Salt Lake, and Young wanted Port to testify that the Mormons, under Young's leadership, could cut that time significantly, perhaps by as much as 20 days.

Getting up in front of the legislature was not nearly so difficult for Port as speaking in church. He didn't have to talk about religion or philosophy, or any other subject where his inability to read made him feel inadequate. He was talking about horses and men traveling between Salt Lake and Missouri, a subject he knew as much about as any man alive. He said if there were supply stations every 50 to 100 miles, stocked with plenty of oats, where a man driving a light carriage could change horses, a man with a good team could cover 150 miles a day in good weather. Under these conditions the mail might make it to Salt Lake in 15 days. Another seven days would put it in Sacramento.

The legislature authorized Brigham Young to personally outfit and build the supply stations between Salt Lake and Fort Laramie. Young founded the Brigham Young Express and Carrying Company, soon known to all as the YX Company. Men were called on building missions to construct the supply stations.

In April Port was asked to be guide and hunter for a delegation of local politicians traveling to Washington to pitch the new mail contract. Also in the group were apostles and missionaries heading on church missions. A.O. Smoot was captain.

Assembling for departure at the mouth of Emigration Canyon, on the exact spot where Port had sliced off Silas Boyle's head, Brigham Young blessed each of the men that their missions would be successful.

A short distance east of Fort Bridger the party came to an abrupt halt as a major blizzard swept in from the north, bringing with it heavy snows and freezing winds that didn't let up for almost three days.

The storm caught the party in the middle of the open prairie, where the men quickly pitched their tents and crawled inside to wait out the late winter wrath. Port didn't sleep as well as the rest, getting up periodically to check the horses. Spring had come early in the Salt Lake Valley, and the horses had already begun to shed their winter coats.

With their backs to the wind and their heads down, the horses seemed to be surviving. But on Port's third trip out of the tent, he noticed one of the animals lying down. He could not make it get up. He noticed that two of the others were acting like they wanted to lie down too.

"The horses are freezing," Port shouted. "Bring me your blankets." The men began to stir. Some complained about coming outside in the storm.

"Bring me the blankets." Port shouted again

"How will we keep warm?" someone shouted back.

"Put on your coat."

"Never took it off."

In the midst of the howling storm the men stumbled among the horses, tying on blankets as best they could. If it hadn't been for the wind the task would have been easy. When the men took off their gloves to tie the knots, their fingers froze. They had no wood for fires. For the remainder of the night the men huddled together in the tents, occasionally checking the horses, Praying for the storm to subside. But it paid little heed.

At first light they stumbled through three miles of blowing snow to the nearest grove of trees. Here the horses found some relief from the relentless wind. The men found all the firewood they needed to maintain roaring campfires for the duration of the storm.

The grove was a mixture of cottonwood and fir trees. While the fir offered the most protection against the bitter wind, the smaller cottonwood branches provide marginal nourishment for the hungry horses.

On the third day the storm blew itself out and the party continued on its way, wading through the deep snow. But it was May, and when the sun finally appeared, it was high in the sky, reflecting so brightly off the thick snow that the men could hardly see. With black ashes rubbed around their eyes, they looked like raccoons. Still, the May sun was too bright, and by the end of the second day, the party had to halt because half the men were snow-blind and simply could not see to travel.

While they were recovering, Indians ran off a dozen horses in broad daylight. Port galloped after them on his stallion. He returned two days later with six of the stolen animals.

The party had to wait out two more storms. But by the end of May the men were riding through green grass, eating fresh buffalo meat, and passing emigrant trains almost hourly. They reached the Big Blue in Missouri ten day ahead of schedule.

Except for the Indians stealing their horses near Fort Laramie, there were few problems with the red men, but that was to change quickly.

East of Fort Laramie a cow wandered away from a company of Danish emigrants right into a Sioux camp. Seeing breakfast on the hoof, the Indians quickly killed the cow and proceeded to prepare a feast.

The Danish brother who lost the cow reported the incident to the officer in charge at Fort Laramie, Lieutenant John Gratten, who dispatched 29 soldiers to ride with him to teach the Sioux a lesson. The Indians saw the soldiers coming, prepared an ambush, and slaughtered all 29 cavalrymen.

When news of the massacre reached General William Harney, he marched with several hundred men on the Sioux camp. Upon discovering that the braves were absent, he proceeded with the attack anyway, slaughtering 80 women and children, thus earning his nickname, Squaw Killer Harney.[6]

---

[6]   Storm Testament 6, Lee Nelson, pp. 381

A NEW START

Ike felt like somehow he needed to get past this haze he was in. He had been so devastated by the passing of Mary and how dare Elmer talk about being sealed to Mary. What a ridiculous idea. He had given Mary plenty of leeway to marry Elmer if she had wanted to. He would have stepped out of the way, but she hadn't wanted Elmer and then for Elmer to bring up her being sealed to him right after she had died. He wondered if Elmer had any sense of propriety in his being. The least he could have done is waited for a while. He was in the depths of despair when he had said that, how could he. Unbelieveable. Ike was looking for an answer to his loss and he met two young ladies that seemed interested in him. They were named Amelia Brown and Harriet Gully. He knew if he married them that others might feel that he was trying to replace Mary and in a way he was. He just couldn't seem to get past her loss. There so seemed no end to the pain. He married both of them in 1856. Maybe he was tried to heal from the devastation. He had discussed it at some length with Aseneth and she had liked having the extra help and the company when he was gone. She liked both of them and hoped a fast relationship would grow. Even if they weren't quite as easy to get along with, she could make it work. No one would be as easy to get along with as Mary. They had been best friends for what seemed like forever. She would always miss Mary and there would always be a place in her heart for her no matter who else she learned to love. She knew Ike felt the same way. She had sensed how very dear Mary was to Ike and she had been very sensitive to Ike about that loss. She also sensed that Ike had married the two other girls to help get over his loss.

Well, now he had picked two new wives it came down to working all of it out. They sat down in a family counsel and talked about their various chores. It seemed like both of his new wives were ready to go with their new responsibilities and Aseneth seemed happy with the arrangement. She still had control of the kitchen which delighted her and both of her new sisters were quite willing to step into the kitchen when there seemed like a lot to do. Amelia had been willing to help out with outside chores when Ike was gone. She said she loved being outdoors and was delighted with that responsibility. It looked like things would go very smoothly. Ike when he was home liked to sit down with the girls and he and Aseneth's baby and discuss whatever was on their minds at the time. Ike hoped it wouldn't turn out to be a complaint session for any of the girls. He crossed his fingers that wouldn't be what these get-togethers would be about. He played with Emily whenever he had time, but there were things to be done. He had fences to fix and hay to get put up. He wanted to get up into the mountains soon and see how his friends, the Indians, were doing.

Harriet seemed a little spoiled, and he and Aseneth sensed that early on. They decided the best way to handle that was not to notice every little complaint she made. When she brought things up that she wanted to be different, he and Aseneth would try their best to meet her halfway. They felt that if they babied her they would encourage any sourness and so they proceeded with that system of handling her. It seemed to be working and they went on with their lives.

As they talked one night and Ike played with Emily he mentioned he would be going out to hunt tomorrow.

"Do you have to go," said Harriet. "It gets so lonely when you are gone. Couldn't you postpone it for a week or so."

"There will be a lot of times when I have to be gone. You should be fine with Aseneth and Amelia around to keep you company. You love to play with Emily."

"I know, but it's not the same as when you are here.

"You need to try to get used to it. There will so many times in the future that I will have to gone. I am sorry, but that is just how it will have to be. I promise I will always hurry back to you."

"Okay, I will try to get used to it, but no promises."

"Well, as long as you will try. That will be okay."

Ike's eyes met Aseneth's and he could tell exactly what she was thinking, something like "Ahhh, poor little baby." He sensed a need to discuss it with Aseneth. He motioned for Aseneth to meet him outside.

"I sure miss how it was with you and Mary, never a complaint. You were fine with letting me go and you always met me outside when I came back with a big smile on your faces. I hope this gets better. I hate to have her dragging on me every time when it's time to go. I just feel that not only do I have to hunt, but my friends in the mountains need me to. I hope to be there for them when the times get tough. I don't know how much I can do, but I have to try."

"I truly understand and we knew up front exactly what was to be expected of us. I think that was part of the reason that Mary requested that we all three marry the same time. She was a pretty smart cookie."

"Yes, she was. When she first said only if you marry my best friend, I thought it sounded strange. I couldn't understand what she meant, but now there is just the two of us left from the original marriage, I totally understand. She knew what she was doing. I better quit talking about her or it will bring tears to my eyes again."

"I know, me too. Let's celebrate her with some cookies when you come back. I got hungry for them when we were just talking."

"You silly girl, talking about Mary being a smart cookie shouldn't have made you hungry for cookies. I guess we are getting past the worst pain of losing her, if we can laugh about it."

"That I think is good. We have to move on and that's how to do it."

"I just want you to know how much I appreciate you, Aseneth. You are the stalwart in my life. You always seem to have the best ideas. I am growing to love you more every day."

"Thanks, Ike, little things like that you say keep me going. A little thing like that will fuel me for weeks."

"Thanks Aseneth. You are a sweetheart, truly a sweetheart."

They went back into the house.

Ike rose early the next morning and was gone. He thought it best to be up before first light. He didn't want Harriet causing another fuss.

EMILY, AGAIN

Yes, Emily was on his mind again. Porter mind always went back to Emily. He knew wives come and go, but Emily was his blood and she would always be in his heart. Mary Ann was none too happy that Emily was on his mind. She felt like if Emily was on his mind, then Luana was on his mind. He had tried to convince her that wasn't the case, but she hung onto the idea. Porter had let any feelings for Luana go long ago, but convincing Mary Ann of that was another story.

One time when he was in California, he headed eastward toward Salt Lake and he became obsessed with seeing Emily. He turned his horse toward Sacramento bent on taking Emily back to Salt Lake. The miles went quickly and he found her hut on the edge of a cliff. He could see Emily beam when she saw him, but behind the happiness was a coolness that they had unresolved differences. They sat and talked. When Emily saw a different way that his long hair was braided she knew that was Mary Ann's mark. She couldn't get past resenting her Dad's young wife. Henry her husband who had been out panning for gold walked in and sat down. Immediately Porter said, "I've come to take you and Emily back to the valley. I will teach you a way to ensure your future in the horse raising business. You can't plan on staying here scrapping by for a few dollars a day."

"But what if we don't want to go," said Henry as he raised his voice.

"Then I will tie you to a saddle and drag you there." At that point Porter charged Henry and they crashed through a window. Henry went over the cliff and fell into the water 80 feet below. Porter dove into the water after him and pulled him to shore. Porter hit him again and when Emily descended the cliff with a pack horse they took him on the horse back up to the cabin. They returned to their food as nothing had happened. After the meal Porter rode away feeling foolish, but also knowing he had shown Emily how much he cared.

HIS FRIENDS

Ike was missing his friends that he usually found up in the Sanpete area. He felt that these friends would stick by him no matter what came along. It was a nice feeling to know that was true. He thought that if another tribe were attacking him that the local Ute Indians, or at least Blackhawk and his brother Mountain, would help him out.

He had done all he could do to make Harriet happy with his leaving the night before, but he was beginning to learn that she would complain no matter what extra attempts he made to help her understand that there were times when he would have to go over night.

He rode up into the Sanpete valley anxious to hunt with them. They always started their hunt very early in the morning, or at times in the evening just before dusk. He knew that was the best two times to catch the animals out. Elk and deer were nocturnal feeders unless they were very hungry. Then you might find them out any time of the day. He knew if the Indians were too busy today he might have to stay there tonight and plan on a morning hunt. If they had some kind of a project going he would help them with it. He had done that many times before. Most of the projects were the work of the women. The primary responsibility of the men was to bring home food and that lately was getting tougher and tougher. And consequently so were the tempers of the Indians getting shorter and shorter. Blackhawk and his band hadn't yet attacked the whites, but it was getting closer and closer to happening. There had been other attacks in the valley. There had been the incident at Tooele where another band had stolen horses and Porter Rockwell had gone out to find the horses. Ike had heard the few they had captured had led Porter and his group all around and when the Indians pointed back at Tooele so the story goes, Porter had shot all of them except a young one that ran off. Then of course there was the Pahvants that had killed the survey crew down on the Sevier River. The Indians spoke of the bravery of the surveyor leader and how bravely he had fought. The Pahvants had been so impressed they had passed his heart around after his death as each of them took a bite to have a piece of a very brave man.

Ike rode into the Indian camp about noon. A few of the young braves gave Ike a second glance. It looked like they all were getting a little tense with the white man. He found out from one of Blackhawk's wives that Mountain had left early that morning and had been gone all day. She pointed in the general direction he had taken and Ike rode that way. He was quite anxious to get out into the timber and feel the air on his face as he rode. He knew that in that amount of time that Mountain had been gone he could have traveled far from the camp. He might not find him today, and that was okay. Nothing was more enjoyable to him than to spend a night under the stars. He rode in a northeasterly direction checking when he arrived on a ridge in all directions for a sign of the Indians. He jumped a couple of buck deer but he let them go. He didn't want to fall into the trap of taking food from the Indians when they weren't present. He wanted them to be present when he shot a deer or elk. He always shared part of his kill with the Indians and it was better to be with them. He always liked the way an Indian would drop down on one knee and thank the spirit of the animal for the use of his body to feed his family. He sometimes forgot to do that as they had taught him and he didn't want to ever have to lie to the Indians and claim to have done it when he hadn't. He felt it safer for all concerns to just not kill an animal unless some Indians were with him. Lying was one of the major things that Indians never did. The honor of a man was heavily placed on his never lying and he wasn't about to abuse his honor in any way.

As he rode along the top of a ridge he noticed one rider down in a draw. He pulled up and watched the man. At first he wasn't sure if it was a white man or an Indian. He was too far away to be sure. He sat on his horse for a long time watching the man. The man must have seen him and started riding his way. Shortly he could tell it was a white man. He was leading a pack mule. He must have been out for awhile. Soon the rider came closer and closer. There was something familiar about the rider. He wasn't sure if it was the way he rode or if there was something else that made Ike think he knew him. He came up on the ridge cutting back and forth to make the climb easier for his animals. One time as he turned Ike noticed the telltale sign of a braid running down his back. He thought to himself, well, I'll be damned if I haven't run into Porter Rockwell. There was certainly no two men that looked the same when it came to Porter Rockwell. Porter rode right up to Ike.

"Well, I'll be if it isn't Ike Potter. How have you been? I haven't seen you for what two years or more."

"I think it has been all of that. Are they keeping you busy?"

"Busy is an understatement. Guess who is called everytime a stealer steals or a rustler rustles. I'm presently looking for 4 cowboys that took about 20 head from one of your neighbors down in Utah Valley. They were riding a pinto and a paint. They shouldn't be hard to recognize when I find them. Of course many a cowboy had been hung because they were riding the wrong color of horses. It will take a sight more evidence than the color of the horses before I arrest them."

"I hear they saddled you with the job of marshal."

"You know they did, but they just as well had. I get called out by Brigham whether I was marshal or not. I just as well be the marshal."

"I've heard you have been all over the west lately."

"I think you know more about me than I do, but yes, in the last 2 years I've been to California what twice I think. I've been back east several times. I took a bunch of politicians back to Washington D.C. once and I went back there myself. Brigham has been itching to get the Pony Express contract and he sent me back to talk to those politicians about what we could do and how much time it would take to do it. It looks to me like we might get the contract. I tell you my wife Mary Ann sure has a fit when I am gone so much. Say, how are you doing with your two wives. That sure looked like a hornet's nest to me to start out from scratch with twice as many headaches as a normal man has."

"You know, I have thought about what you said last time we talked many times. It was the work of one girl that made all the difference. When I asked her to marry me, she said no unless I would marry her best friend at the same time. That put the fear of all hell in me. I didn't want to start out with two wives. I did not want to do that, but that little lady planned that to a tee. It worked out perfectly. Never a cross work or a complaint the entire time. She had it planned to where she took care of the kitchen and the other one took care of the rest. It worked perfectly and neither of them ever complained when I left or how long I was gone. When I got back each time they both met me out front with big smiles on their faces. It was unbelievable how well it worked."

"You keep talking about how well it worked as if it has changed now. Is there something different?"

"Its still hard to talk about. The one I asked to marry first, the one that organized the whole thing died in child birth a little over a year ago."

"I was so affected by it all that I tried to replace her with two others and then my problems began. The one, Amelia, is doing fine, but the other one is a little spoiled and she is a handful. I really wonder if that wasn't a huge mistake."

"You know, I have been all over the country in the last 2 years and it sounds like you have covered more ground than me. When they start complaining about your absence, I don't think that ever changes. I sure have my hands full with my wife and her complaining and the biggest trouble is I love it out here under the stars at night and the smell of sage the rest of the time. I love it and no one can take that away from me. It's built into me."

"You know, I feel exactly the same way. I love it out here. I just wish there were more game left. The Indians are a boiling keg about to boil over. I spend quite a bit of time with Blackhawk and his brother and all hell will break loose one of these days. I wish we had had the foresight to have done things differently, but now I think it is a little too late. It is getting tense."

"You know of anybody I know you probably have a better handle on what is going on with the Indian than anybody else. It was good to talk to you. Your name will probably come up the next time I talk to Brigham. Not that it will make any difference, I, as you, think it is a little too late to change anything. It will get tough real soon. I need to get on my way. Have you seen anything of those boys that I am looking for?"

"I've only been out here for a few hours, but haven't seen anyone until you. Good luck with them. Don't let them get the drop on you."

"You never know when it is our time, but so far, no one's got me. Knock on wood. I've guess I will have to use my head. It's the only wood I have near."

Porter rode off back in the same direction that he had been going. As he rode away, Ike thought about the time when he wondered if he would ever get to know The Porter Rockwell. Now I guess I am past that day. We had a good conversation and he looked forward to more.

FRANK SLADE

Porter was once again a mess over Emily. Emily had come back to the Salt Lake Valley after Henry had died of the fever. Porter had been so glad to see her, but still hurt over her rejecting him in California. He had had very mixed feelings when it came to Emily. She had also totally rejected Mary Ann. She just couldn't let it go that she inwardly still hoped that her father and her mother Luana would somehow get back together. She and Mary Ann had had hard words several times and Emily had refused to move back into Porter's cabin even though Mary Ann had moved back to her mom and dad's place for a time. Emily had a good heart, but some things continued to overpower her choices.

Porter had used a dry well to bury some of the outlaws that he had had to kill. Emily found out about the dry well and couldn't let her disgust over it be forgotten. One day she left a note for Porter and disappeared again. The note said she was going back to California again, breaking her dad's heart one more time.

'In a tavern down on the Mexican border the owner of the tavern challenged the men there to see if any of them could handle the Mormon lawmen in Utah. He put up some money on the bar and challenged anyone to match it. Several of the customers matched his money, but there seemed to be no takers to go to Utah and take on Rockwell. For a time no one took on the challenge, then a man stepped forward, matched the money, had the owner hold the kitty and swore that he would return with the head of Porter Rockwell.

Frank Slade rode north with all the confidence possible that he would kill Porter Rockwell and return with the proof that he had done the deed. After arriving in Salt Lake he became involved with the local judge, Drummond, and he was asked to lay low for some months. Judge Drummond wanted to use the assassination of Porter to his benefit to topple Brigham Young and become the political power in Salt Lake.

'The agonizing years of laboring at meaningless jobs before finding his niche at killing marshals was now a memory of Slade's about which he'd just as soon forget. Now in the next few moments he was about to experience the greatest satisfaction of his career via the most significant confrontation of his life. While he had spent considerable time studying his prey and waiting for Drummond to give him the word, like a rattlesnake waiting to make his strike, his kitty had dramatically increased through visits to numerous territorial taverns, convincing its participants to float him credit on the bet. He had in fact made a comfortable living at similar bets before bagging other marshals, only this was the only lawman he had ever faced who had inspired ballads to be sung about him at literally dozens of campfires throughout the territory, the lyrics of which were becoming memorized by more than a few:

"They say that Porter Rockwell
Is a scout for Brigham Young
He's hunting up the unsuspects
That haven't yet been hung,
So if you steal one Mormon girl
I'll tell you what to do.
Get the drop on Porter Rockwell
Or he'll get the drop on you."

Slade smiled as he thought of the lyrics. A Mormon girl from the nearest homestead would be his reward, he figured, within minutes even. It was the only kind of girl he had not had, he mused, but would soon be history.

"What can I do for you?" said Porter atop his buckboard.

"I've come clear from a bar on the Mexican border to settle something with you. And I've been following you longer, off and on, than I care to admit."

"Oh?"

Slade pulled a revolver from behind his hat on the saddle horn.

Porter held back his surprise and kept his voice casual. "What's that for?"

"A lot of people want to see you dead," said Slade.

"Is that a fact?"

"A well known fact."

"I'm flattered."

"You should be, so I reckon it's been worth my while to follow you around.'"

"Well this is kinda interesting," said Porter. "Where'd you get this idea?"

"It all started at a bar on the Mexican border. There were some wealthy miners that pitched in. And that's where the biggest kitty lies. There's a lot of cash to get you."

"Thank goodness for that," said Porter. "I'd hate for you to have been following me around for free."

Slade chuckled.

Porter continued, "And worse yet, I'd hate to see you die for free." Both men laughed. Porter read him like a painting and at first he hoped to dissuade him, as he had young Lot Huntington with his ambush attempt, but quickly sized up this fellow as a different species than Lot. This was a cold blooded scorpion. Porter's mind was racing for a solution, realizing within moments that only one of them would be leaving this encounter alive.

"You see," continued Slade, "I reckon a dozen saloons have a kitty riding on the outcome of this here encounter between us."

"I'd sure like a shot at some of those winnings," said Porter.

"How do you reckon that?" said Slade.

"By a fair contest. That way the winner takes all."

Slade smiled, "I think you'll be the one dying, Mr. Rockwell."

"Is that a fact?"

"Soon to be a well known fact."

"Well, now that we have our facts straight," said Porter, "I just need one thing."

"What's that?"

"The address of that Mexican border bar," said Porter.

"I ain't giving you the address to no bar. What do you want with that?" said Slade. "I told you there's no way you're coming out of this alive."

"That's fine with me. I don't want no betting' money; it's against my religion. I need the address for another reason."

"What reason is that?" chuckled Slade.

"Just hypothetically speaking," said Porter, "what if you died?"

Slade laughed back. "First of all, I won't die"

Hypothetically," said Porter.

"All right, hypothetically. So, hypothetically if I die, what do you want the address for?"

"To send your remains." said Porter.

"Mr. Rockwell, "laughed Slade. "That ain't happening. What is happening is this" after our encounter here, I will be showing the whole world your demise."

"Very good." said Porter. "Now what do you plan to do to show you got me?"

Slade smiled as his eyes widened. "Cut off your head and take it off in a bag."

Porter smiled. "Whoee! Grissssley!"

Slade chuckled, taken back by Port's reaction.

"But," said Porter, "let's just pretend for a moment that you don't pull that off."

Slade lost his laughter a moment.

Porter continued smiling. "So what's that address?"

The thought suddenly crossed Slade's mind of what an interesting and humiliating surprise it would be for the bartender and all his friends at the Mexican border bar to open up a parcel only to find Slade's three week old, very ripe remains to both surprise and inform them Slade had lost.

"I don't think so," said Slade. "You don't need their address."

"Wait a second," said Porter, playing out his hand. "How're those fine folks at the border bar ever going to now if, heaven forbid, you lost?" said Porter. "They would be out of their winnings if you didn't return."

"If I lost," said Slade, "they'd hear about it."

"How?"

"You'd tell the newspapers."

"I don't tell the newspapers nothing," said Porter. "Most make up what they print."

"Well I don't really care about that," said "Slade, displaying a faint discomfort. "So let's get on with it."

"Don't you care about what happens to them folks back at the bar?"

"Not really."

"You struck me as an upright fellow," said Porter. "Them folks at the bar deserve some kind of accounting of what happens to you."

"All right, all right!" said Slade animatedly. "If I lose, I lose. But I still don't want you sending my corpse to them. So let's get on with it."

"Wait a minute. Wait a minute," said Porter. "Don't you wanna know the alternative to you being shipped back in a crate?"

"No."

"Well I sure would wanna know what would happen to me if I was you."

"All right, what would happen to me if I didn't get shipped back in a crate?" he said, rolling his eyes.

"The dry well," said Porter.

"What?"

"The dry well."

"Dry well?"

"Dry well."

"What the devil's the dry well?" said Slade.

"Well, it's a secret, basically," said Porter. "But since you're about to end up there, I reckon it won't do no harm to tell you about my secret. Better yet, I could show you."

"No thanks," said Slade.

"Well, have it your way."

"I definitely don't care about your dry _____"

"Don't you want to even see it from a distance?"

"No."

"Okay," said Porter.

"Definitely not."

"You don't know what you're missing. But have it your way."

Where were we?" said Slade.

"It's over there." Porter pointed to the dry well downhill and northwest of them, out in a field. "I know you were dying to know deep inside. Especially … what's in it. Now, weren't you?" said Porter with a smile.

Slade glanced back at the well, beginning to get a little curious." All right … what's in it?"

"Couple dozen corpses of outlaws, I reckon."

"You reckon? You don't know? Who put them there?"

"I suppose it was me," said Porter modestly.

Slade thought a second and tried to conceal his minuscule gulp.

Porter continued, "The flies in that thing have a field day. I reckon the maggots too. The activity in that well is something ferocious, I'd imagine. Can you imagine it?"

Slade just looked at him, thinking.

"Now the bottom of a dry well is an interesting place," added Porter. "Do you like small, deep, deep holes to sit in for a few hundred years?"

Slade was terrified of small places, and the idea completely disconcerted him.

"So." said Porter, "it's your choice. The well or the parcel post to the bar."

"Well, I suppose anything's better than that well," Slade mumbled, daydreaming.

"Now what's that address?" said Porter.

"Miguel's Cantina in Tijuana." Slade suddenly caught himself and jerked out of his reverie, realizing he had been suckered into Porter's mind game, and he smiled.

"You find it funny?" said Porter.

"Yeah, I find you funny."

"Well I reckon you can get on with your business then," said Porter. "Cause I'd hate for one of us to leave this earth without a smile on his face."

"I reckon so," said Slade smiling.

"At least in a minute or two."

"A minute or two?"

"Yeah," said Porter. "But only when your're ready."

"I'm not ready?" said Slade with a sardonic chuckle.

Porter snorted softly.

"What're you laughin' at?" said Slade.

Porter didn't answer. He just snorted.

Slade's laughter suddenly became laced with a tint of seriousness. "Have you ever seen a snake that's been gut-shot, Mr. Rockwell? It squirms in the dust for hours before it dies. I reckon I've done that to a few snakes in my day."

"How many's a few?" said Porter.

"Maybe a half-dozen."

"Well now," said Porter, "you oughta be real proud of yourself. If you've gut-shot half a dozen snakes, I guess I would make an even seven, ain't that right?"

"An even seven?" Slade laughed. "I like you, Marshal. An even seven. Yeah, that's good. That's real good. I do like you."

"Well, I kinda like you too, Slade."

"Yes sir, you got a sense of humor as loco as mine."

"Maybe I am as loco as you," said Porter with a twinkle in his voice.

Slade suddenly lost his smile and trembled a moment, then broke into loud guffaws. "Maybe I oughta just shoot you in the head right now for saying that and be done with it. Nobody ever gets away with calling me loco."

"Naw, that's spoil your fun" said Porter. "You wanna gut-shoot me like them snakes." Porter sensed Slade trembling again with anticipation.

Slade smiled, "I reckon you're right. But all that really matters is to get your head in this bag," he said.

"You could even mount it," said Porter.

Slade broke into laugher again. "That's right ! That's it!" He gasped and panted.

"But what if I get lazy and don't parcel post you back to that bar in Tijuana? It's be real convenient just to dump you with your new acquaintances in the well over there ... all them thousands of maggots and flies and worms and bugs ... millions of bugs. Can you see the well all right from here, Slade?"

Slade nodded.

"On a clear day you can see it 30 miles away. On those days I reckon you can ever see the odor rising out of it."

Slade was contemplative. It hadn't occurred to him anyone had seen odor before.

"Then again," added Porter, "let's hope you're completely dead when I dump you in there. That'd be one horrible place to spend your last hours if you were only wounded. Or to spend days—especially days, huh Slade? Now wouldn't it?"

Porter could see beads of sweat appearing on Slade's forehead. He observed Slade imagining many, many things as he glanced at the dry well in the distance again. Porter continued, "A hundred feet down—two hundred maybe,

maybe even three hundred feet—cold, dark, moist, a million flies, and a billion maggots crawling over you, waiting for you to die, waiting to dig in."

"Dig in?"

"That's awful, huh, Slade?" said Porter.

"Yeah."

"I don't know that much about maggots, do you?"

"No."

"But I reckon that'd be an awful way to go—in that cold …dark … deep, deep hole, where it's a real small room at the bottom, and real disgusting."

Slade felt a sudden nausea in the pit of his stomach.

"So, Slade, when you're ready to shoot it out, just let me know."

Slade said reticently, "I am ready."

Porter smiled, "No you're not."

Slade fought his emotions; he turned his uncertainty into anger. He spat out his words: "Nobody believes God protects you—hair or no hair."

"I never said the hair protects me—though I reckon it's true I won't die because of it."

"How can you say you don't say it when you just said it?"

"Did I?" said Porter.

"What are you—crazy? I just heard you say it!"

"Son of a gun."

"You don't really believe it, though, do you, Rockwell?" smiled Slade, trying to regain control.

"Maybe I do, maybe I don't. But the important thing," said Porter, reading Slade's slightly dilated eye, "is that you do."

"That is loco!"

"I suppose it does sound that way, don't it? There you sit, looking at me, wondering if I am going to live through this fight because of my hair. Now being a good, Bible-reading Christian such as yourself, Slade, I'm sure you've heard of Samson."

"That's Bible story stuff and it's double loco."

"May be, Slade, but you believed it when your mama read you the Good Book as a boy. So now, here you are, face to face with some creature—namely me—and the little kid in you is probably saying, "Goodness gracious, this fellow looks like that creature who took apart the Philistines ... and there's only one of me. Ain't that right, Slade?"

"Looks mean nothing," shot back "Slade. "You and Brigham believing that trash proves you're both loco."

"I ain't convinced you're convinced of that, Slade."

"Well no matter, cause I'm gonna kill you anyway." Slade was one second away for cocking his pistol when Porter stated, "Slade ... there's one other reason you can't kill me."

"You can't shoot that thing without a cap."

"What?"

"That shot doesn't have a cap on it," said Porter, "and the next cylinder to chamber also has no cap on it."

Slade thought a long, tense moment ...While it was common to have the percussion cap fall off the nipple of a cap and ball revolver—simply because of the slight friction fit that could easily be bounced loose, and at one point his pistol had jarred against his rifle when he had mounted his horse—he also knew Porter was probably bluffing to get the drop on him. He could see Porter's Colt Navy stuck tightly in his belt, so it would take Porter two seconds to get off a shot. Still, he could not take chances. There was no way on earth this conniving marshal was going to trick him into looking down.

Yet, the marshal seemed awfully serious about what he was saying, and Slade had learned from many a poker game how to read faces. The more Slade thought about it—and the more he tried reading Porter's eyes—the more he began weighing the possibility that Porter was telling the truth. Why would Porter tell the truth? He asked himself. The marshal needed the challenge, he mused, and didn't want his opponent so easily taken down.

Then the worst thing that could happen happened. He noticed Porter's eyes laughing. Porter would draw his own Colt Navy any second, and here Slade would be caught naked with no percussion cap! He knew he had to do something—he kept spare caps in the tin in his vest pocket—but from timing himself previously he knew it would take nine seconds to take out the tin, grab a cap, and get it on the one nipple. A second alternative would be to grab a second loaded and primed cylinder in his pocket and place it in his Colt—and that would take just seven and a half seconds and also buy him a guaranteed six shots if needed. But the third and best alternative hit him—he could grab his loaded rifle latched to the saddle with a quick release—and within two seconds he would have a shot off. But, he would have a hundred percent chance for a kill if he simply had the percussion cap on his Colt Army in the first place! He had to know if the cap was there. He could not lose the precious second looking at the cap—or even attempting to fire—If he could be going for his rifle. Was Porter tricking him or not! He squinted harder, trying to read Porter's eyes further. Then he saw Porter turn serious. He finally figured him out! Port was telling the truth!

Then Porter really threw him. "Then, again, maybe you do have a cap."

From the look in Porter's eyes, he was on the verge of pulling out his own Colt. Panicked, Slade felt his face flush. He had to act fast. He had to first check the cap, and if it weren't there—which it probably wasn't—he would grab the rifle.

He glanced down at his Colt Army to if the cap was there. Porter was wrong! It was there! Relieved, Slade looked up again, ready to blow the marshal away, when he found himself staring straight into porter's Colt Navy.

A split second later he found himself staring at a flash coming from Porter's Colt Navy.

"How did he pull that thing so fast?" thought Slade, flying backwards through the air.

Seconds later he saw barren desert dirt at close range. He was lying face down, sprawled across the road, staring into his own blood soaking in the sand. Then he looked up and saw fluffy white clouds in the clear blue sky.

"Good," he groaned, "shot."

"How did I draw so fast, you're thinking?" said Porter. "Well, I'll tell you. You saw my Colt Navy stuck in my belt, but you didn't see my other one in my left hand under my coat. A lot of people don't know this, but Brigham gave me a pair of these beauties. Don't you think that was a good idea?"

"Yep," mumbled Slade.

Porter noticed Slade staring up at him, then at the clouds again. "It's a beautiful day," added Slade, "to die."

"I reckon."[7]

---

[7]   The Porter Rockwell Chronicles, Richard Lloyd Dewey, pp. 415.

THE MAIL

When Porter returned to Salt Lake in November he had a new baby girl. She was named Sarah. Later that year Porter homesteaded some land in Government Creek and some in Cherry Creek. He built a cabin to stay in when he was on the land. He didn't move Mary Ann and the two little girls. He wanted them safe in town. The Indians were beginning to cause problems and he didn't want them out there. Porter wondered where the Indian problems would stop. The Indians were getting a real attitude over the loss of game to feed their families.

Porter bought 16 acres for $500 near the point of the mountain south of Salt Lake near a hot spring. He built an inn and took in two partners. Charles Mogo was a brewer and David Burr was a builder. Construction began immediately. The brewery was capable of producing 500 gallons of lager beer a day. Porter thought soldiers and teamsters would be his most frequent customers.

That next winter YX Company was awarded with the mail contract from San Francisco to Independence, Missouri. Porter was assigned from Salt Lake to Fort Laramie. The first time the mail took 40 days to arrive. The route wasn't very well prepared. Horse weren't ready at the stations, the weather wasn't helpful, snow and rain. Sometimes the station managers weren't even present when the mail arrived. The first trip took 40 days. The next time they made sure everything was ready and it took 15 days. The YX company was a success.

On one trip Porter was told a company of soldiers were enroute to remove Brigham Young from Salt Lake. Porter and two others hurried to Salt Lake to tell Brigham what was happening. Immediate measures were taken to slow the movement of the soldiers. The federal troops entailed 2500 soldiers and 2 batteries of artillery. It was known as Johnston's Army.

Daniel H. Wells of the Nauvoo Legion was ordered to engage the enemy before they entered the valley. Porter Rockwell, Bill Hickman and Lot Smith were picked to lead the harassment efforts. Their orders were clear not to kill any of the soldiers, only to harass their movements in any way possible. Porter, Hickman and Smith found the army near South Pass. They watched them from a near hill deciding the best tactics to make their lives as miserable as possible.

"Well, what do you think, brothers? What is the best way to make it as hard as possible for these troops to make it to Salt Lake," whispered Porter.

"Taking away their horses and mules certainly would make it tough for them. They can't do a thing with those cannons and wagons without their animals, returned Bill.

"You notice that long rope down the middle of those tents. Do you suppose they tie their horses there at night?

See those grain pans along that rope. It must be what they do," said Porter. "I think we need to help those horses have a little freedom tonight. It must be very bothersome to have to stand there at that rope all night long."

After dark they slipped down and cut the lead ropes of all of the animals. Just before first light when all the ropes had been cut they rode along both sides of the picket rope and chased all the animals out of the camp. When they checked they had over 2,000 horses and mules moving toward Salt Lake. They stopped for a short break and they heard a bugle sound. It was the sound to announce the arrival of oats for all the animals. Before they knew it all the horses and mules run back for their parcel of oats. They had all been on foot and even their saddle horses were gone. There they stood on foot wondering what to do.

After dark they moved quietly toward the huge army camp. The found a small group of saddled horses and they quickly led them away. When they arrived at Daniel Wells' camp they were told they had found the horses of another harassing group of Mormons that were also assigned to cause havoc to the soldiers. That left those Mormons on foot dangerously close to the enemy. Port, Bill and Hickman felt a little silly but knew it was a little late to fix their mistake now.

The troopers began blaming the harassments on the Mormon Dannites. The harassers stampeded their animals, stole their supplies with hit and run tactics. They began preparing Echo Canyon with trenches to shoot from, bounders to roll on the soldiers and tricks to run flood waters down on the soldiers. Later when it was appraised they felt they had burned 500,000 pounds of provisions for the soldiers. Fort Bridger was burned to the ground and later when Jim Bridger saw the destruction, he knew it was the Mormons and he was none too happy.

"Would you look at that? You have got to be kidding me. Those damn Mormons have burned the Fort. Those Mormons have been a thorn in my side for some time. They built another store not too far from here and left me only the Indians to trade with. Those thieves and robbers, I used to think they were a decent lot, but my opinion is changing every day. How dare they do this to me," said Jim Bridger. "This time they have dug me a hole it will be hard to climb out of. I wished they hadn't done this."

"They have proved themselves to be a tough bunch. I can't believe the things they have done to us, just to slow us down. I think they burned the Fort because you were guiding us. Maybe they were not too happy that you were helping us out," said the soldier standing by Jim.

"Maybe so, but that doesn't make me any happier with them burning the Fort. They surely could have thought of something else to burn."

Jim Bridger shouldn't have felt too bad because they burned Fort Supply also. There were over 100 cabins there that were burned as well.

Wells and his men burned grass in front of troops to slow them down. They stampeded a herd of nearly 2400 cattle that was winter food for the troops. They took most of the cows back to Salt Lake as winter set in. They were pretty sure the troops would have to wait out the winter before entering the Salt Lake valley. The Mormons went home for the winter driving the stolen cattle before them.

ATTITUDE

Ike rode back into the Indian camp not too long before dark. When he got there both Mountain and Blackhawk were back. Mountain had been hunting all day and Blackhawk had been to an Indian parlay. Mountain hadn't had much success but was willing to try it again and Ike was invited to ride with them.

Blackhawk discussed the meeting he had been to that day and was willing to talk about it. He said most of the other groups were near a boiling point and Ike knew that meant more attacks on the whites. Ike didn't add any negative ideas about attacking the whites. He knew his hands were tied to help on either side. He did say he would talk to some of the bishops in the area and try to get them to share some of their cattle. He was appreciated for his help and he had been in the Indian camp enough that they almost treated him as an Indian. They felt a definite kinship to Ike and he appreciated that. He almost felt that they expected him to fight the whites when the time came. Ike knew he could never shoot a white, but there were many other ways he could help without killing.

Ike rode the next day with Mountain and some others. Mountain had an area he wanted to try. He, as all the Indians, was concerned since the number of game animals was so low, in taking the last of the deer and elk and having no animals for a new crop next year. They were careful to never take more than they needed. Both Ike and the Indians knew it was too bad that too many of the animals had already been taken, so if they only saw a few in the area they would never take the last of the animals. That was another reason Ike didn't like to kill any game when the Indians weren't there. He looked to their opinion always to see if there were enough animals to produce next year's crop before any game was taken. There were many reasons why Ike killed only with the Indians' okay. The Indians always shared with him. They knew he had a family to feed as well. Indians were never selfish with those who respected the right way to take care of the herds for next year's harvest. They rode most of the day before they finally felt there were enough animals to take some. They harvested 3 bucks. They also knew a few bucks were enough to take care of many does and still have an adequate crop for next year, but in some areas there was hardly any animals left to be managed and all of them knew the reason for that. It was the overkilling of the game animals by the whites. Each area they rode through Ike could feel the tension grow just a little when they realized that area was already over harvested by the whites. It was almost as if there was a change in their posture indicating a greater tension as they rode through yet a new area that was over harvested. It hurt Ike to the core each time he experienced the areas where there were hardly any game left. He had hoped some time ago that this would be avoided. He had hoped that somehow Brigham would stop this senseless killing before it was too late and the Indians were done understanding the ways of the whites. Ike was beginning to feel it was a little too late to make any difference now. There had been too much damage done by the whites.

Ike took the buck half that he was given and headed for home. When he got there Aseneth and Amelia came out to greet him. He was very excited to see them and the children. Harriet was nowhere to be seen.

"I don't see Harriet," said Ike. "What is she doing?"

"You know Harriet," returned Aseneth. "Who knows. She hasn't been a whole lot of help today. She always has something else to do that just can't wait."

"She didn't help much in the kitchen either, but we aren't coming to you with complaints. That isn't what you need to come back to. It is just really good to have you back," said Amelia. "Since there is just the three of us, I want to thank you for making me feel like I am loved and appreciated. Both of you. I know that replacing Mary was almost impossible, but you have both made me feel loved and accepted. I know it was hard for you to not have Ike Junior here, but somehow it would have been hard for all of us. He was a constant reminder of Mary and I would never hold that against him, but for now, it was easier for me."

"For now, ….he is my son, and I will never forget that. For now it was best and Mom and Dad seem like they totally understand. He is just becoming part of their family."

By that time, Amelia had brought a son into their family. Charley was born on April 24, 1857 and Harriet had had a little girl. Their family was growing with leaps and bounds. They all knew or suspected that Harriet was pregnant again and they acknowledged that that was probably part of her being irresponsible.

By the time the first little girl of Harriet's was big enough to walk by herself, they knew she was pregnant. She was showing a stomach that proved that. One day Harriet just disappeared. She had packed a few things during the night and left a note that said, "I tried all, but I'm just not happy here. I need a place that the sun shines all of the time, not just in the summer. Tell Ike I am sorry, but if I'm not happy then I can't make anyone else happy and I like to be happy all of the time. Harriet."

At first it was a shock to all, but soon they all felt like, maybe it was for the best. They knew she was never happy here and like she said, she wanted to be happy all of the time. Of course the others knew that if you need to be happy all the time, you will always be unhappy. You make your own happiness. It doesn't fall out of a tree one day.

THE CALIFORNIANS

When Porter returned to Salt Lake he took some time to spend with his family. He always enjoyed coming home. He loved Mary Ann and enjoyed his time with his children. It wasn't long until Brigham had another problem.

There were 6 Californians being held in house arrest in a hotel. They were gamblers from California bent on meeting the troops on their way to the Salt Lake Valley. They were intent on making the money that could be made from the troops waiting to get to Salt Lake. Brigham didn't want them to stay in the valley, but he didn't want them either to go the troops and tell them what was to be seen in Salt Lake. He really wanted them gone. With them came the elements of gambling that follows gambling houses; houses of prostitution, drinking establishments and other problems that henceforth he had been able to keep out of the valley. All six were heavily armed and that also meant trouble.

The decision was made that four of the Californians were to return to California. The other two were allowed to stay if they became part of the local residents and did not begin starting a gambling house. Port and three others were assigned to get them back to California.

They stopped in Nephi the first night. The Californians had become quite friendly and seemed fine with the need to return to California. They even asked to stand guard. During the night his dog as he had done many times before licked his face signaling there was something not right. He had trained his dog to do that and not bark, just lick his face. He rose with a steel picket pin and his revolver to see what was happening. He found the Californians getting ready to leave. As he neared the horses he heard whispering. He then knew it was white men. Indians would never whisper in this situation. He then realized they were taking all the horses. At that point a shotgun was fired into the blankets where Port had lied only moments before. Port now knew they had intended to kill him. He waded into them swinging the pin and shooting his revolver.

When the dust cleared, two of the Californians were dead, one shot and the other with his head cracked open. Two of them were gone. After daylight they rode back into Nephi to find one of the desperadoes in a hotel with a bullet in his back and his head cracked open. Later that day the other one staggered into town. It was never reported to the sheriff, but later outside of Nephi they were ambushed by a spring and their bodies thrown into the water.

When spring arrived Salt Lake was prepared to be burned to the ground. The city that had taken 10 years to build was ready to be burned.

A politician entered Salt Lake in April and Brigham turned over the official seal of the territory to the new governor, Alfred Cumming and the city was saved from burning. Also the agreement was made to place the army headquarters 40 miles from the city. Peace was achieved with few causalities and the Mormons were granted amnesty for stopping Johnston's Army the previous year.

Porter's Inn was in a perfect place to rest troopers on their way into the city. With the arrival of the soldiers and Camp Floyd came all the rough elements that Brigham had guarded against. With it came prostitutes, gamblers, preachers and saloon keepers. They set up establishments almost overnight. Porter's business thrived. It was a perfect stopping off place for travelers.

LOT HUNTINGTON

L ot Huntington was the boy that had stolen from a merchant in town and then tried to turn outlaw. He had been challenged on the Mexican border to kill Porter a few years ago. He had come to the valley fully intending to make a mark for himself as a desperado and kill Porter. Porter had talked him into being his assistant in returning a kidnapped girl to her parents. Lot had worked off his debt to society on Porter's ranch and Porter had become quite fond of him. Lot returned to his desperado ways and he and two others had stolen a horse. Porter, Lot Smith and Ballard had cornered Lot and his outlaw friends in a building and during a shootout all of the three outlaws were killed. Porter had felt the pain of the events because Lot had become his friend and he had had to shoot him.

Upon returning to Salt Lake Porter was summoned by Brigham Young who had a letter sent from California that told a story that sent Porter into an emotional spiral he had never felt before. Apparently Emily was missing and thought dead after her husband had been killed by Indians. Nothing could have hurt Porter more than the news that Emily was dead. Porter stumbled away hurt to the core.

Outside there was a celebration going on and Porter wandered into it.

'Down the first block he walked, then another. Smoke was filling the entire merchant section as fireworks exploded in the air behind him. Through the fog-like smoke he caught sight of someone who faintly reminded him of Emily. He could not tell who it was, but from wisps of partial clearings in the fireworks fog—and with dozens of children whizzing excitedly past in front of him—he caught enough of the woman's identity to realize it was someone he knew.

She also spotted him, and walked quickly toward him, dodging the increasing numbers of latecomers passing between her and him on their way to the fireworks.

"The woman finally arrived before him and stopped. She and Porter stared at each other.

"Porter?" said the woman.

Porter continued gazing at her.

"Do you remember me? I'm Luana's cousin, Julia"

Porter was astonished at how much she resembled both Luana and Emily. At that moment he realized how closely Emily mirrored her mother's image when Luana was in her 20s. He had almost forgotten what Luana looked like, so complete had been his erasure of bittersweet memories.

As the woman spoke, Porter saw her lips moving but did not hear a word. Then the fireworks momentarily paused.

"Would you? She said as the only sentence Porter heard.

"I'm sorry," said Porter. "What did you say?"

"I said, I'm just passing through here on my way to California, where I'll be living with one of my daughters."

"Have you seen her?" said Porter.

"Who?" said the woman. "What're you talking about?"

"Luana."

"Not since Iowa. You know she moved to Minnesota."

Porter was disappointed the woman had no more news of Luana.

"Anyway, I want to know if you'll take on my second cousin—she's a delightful young woman—to raise."

"What?" said Porter.

"Can you take on one of my second cousins? She's still but a child in many ways but is growing up fast."

Shaking his head slowly, still stunned over the news of Emily and now with his senses dulled by the smoke and pounding fireworks resuming in the sky, he mumbled, "I don't know. This might be kinda hard since I've remarried. I've got a new family, Julia."

At that moment, a young lady emerged from the crowd and Porter stared at her, astonished.

The woman who had been talking with Porter finally beamed with a big smile and proclaimed" "Meet my second cousin. Porter, you've got to bone up on family trees. We're talking about your daughter …Emily!"

Porter walked forward toward Emily a few steps, too over whelmed to believe what he was seeing.

Music suddenly struck up by a band two blocks away, as torches were lit across the city in unison.

Thousands of people arose from the wide city sidewalks and poured onto the streets, dancing to wild fiddle and harmonica music. Porter continued walking forward toward his daughter, then saw her burst into tears and raise her arms toward her father.

He saw her mouth the words, "Papa," but did not hear a sound from her because of the cheering and dancing, whooping, and hollering and music filling the air.

At that moment he slowed his walk toward Emily, stopped before her … and hugged her.

She cried in his arms like a little girl. Then he heard a dog barking and looked down. There stood Ugly, old grey Ugly, beside Emily.

Emily's cousin laughed through her tears at the scene, hoping the small ruse she had played—about her second cousin—had not teased Porter too terribly. She had not known—nor did Emily—of the report that Emily was no doubt dead.

Porter said, "Brigham just read me a letter from Linda Carol."

Emily gasped. "Everyone must think I'm dead."

Porter nodded, and with a faint smile said, "Can I pinch you—just to see you're not a ghost?"

"As long as it's not too hard."

Julia now spoke. "Emily was taken by Indian braves who killed her husband, and they traded her—and the dog that she wouldn't let go—to white scouts up on the Humboldt River. One of 'em was my cousin, and he brought her to my wagon train. Life indeed had interesting twists and turns."

Tears streamed down her face as she saw Porter and Emily hugging each other harder amidst the celebrating and dancing.

Ugly jumped up and barked, and Porter laughed. When he had sent Ugly to California he was certain he'd never see him again.

As Julia walked downstreet alone, she looked back through the dancing crowds and spotted Porter and Emily still hugging, then together they hugged the big black dog.

The thought crossed her mind that it was a moment neither would soon forget…

The crowds had mostly drifted home, leaving just several hundred people milling about in the moonlight. Porter and Emily walked together to a small fountain near the street and sat on a bench. Porter held Ugly with one arm and with the other waved at a couple friends, then turned to his daughter with a mile.

"So with three husbands behind you," said Porter, "are you finally going to pack that marrying stuff in?"

"I believe so," said Emily, smiling. "In any case, I don't think I'll be leaving town again. Is that cabin built for me yet?"

"It is, but I hope you'll sell it and move closer to Mary Ann and me. I've even dug a little creek off the main stream, and put your favorite chair beside it—just like the way you have it in the painting—right beside the rushing waters."

Emily's eyes filled with tears.

"I couldn't take it, seeing David killed—'cause I loved him the most. I really loved him." Her eyes glistened in the light. "But I have a comfort I haven't known before—I know we'll be together again—if I live worthy of him, and I get us sealed in the temple. He was a worthy and faithful man."

Porter felt tears of compassion welling up, as well as a strong gratitude that she had deepened her appreciation for the Plan of Salvation.

Emily continued, "You probably don't know this, but Mary Ann and I have been writing, and we've gotten a good friendship going. We also got you figured out a little bit, I think."

"I like all that going on behind my back," he said dryly. "But I ain't sure I wanna know." Ugly jumped on the bench beside him and seemed mesmerized by the lights reflecting off the fountain water streaming in the air.

"Ugly don't seem to be in a hurry to go nowhere, so I reckon I'll be hearing it after all," he smiled.

"It's not all bad," she smiled. "I've put pieces together—and so has she. We may be wrong, but we figure a lot of what you are comes from Joseph. I've heard you talk in your sleep about him. And it's no secret about you blaming yourself for his death and wanting to somehow help out the Saints even harder after he was killed. But what is new to me—what we have figured out about you—goes deeper than that. And some of it goes back to your own pa. He was a sweet man and always gave you everything you needed, even in your younger years—except attention. I've heard you say that much."

Porter studied her in the light reflected from the lanterns beside the fountains. Additional light was filled in by the moon and stars.

Emily continued, "As a kid you wanted to be with him. But he was always taking off to explore and hunt, leaving your ma and his kids. Just as his pa had before him. Burt later he did settle down as he grew older. I've heard all that from your other family members back in Nauvoo. I suppose you felt hurt he left you like that. I reckon it hurt a lot your whole life, because you adored him so much. And I think you've felt alone deep down ever since—and hurt. But at the same time it wrote a map inside you that you probably can't even remember being written. I can imagine you probably always wanted to go hunting and fishing with him more than anything in the world. But he pushed you aside as he'd head out the house for one trip after another. But when I was young, you'd at least take me. So you got rid of some of that map that had been written. But you still left the other kids—and Ma—time and time again. So I believe that is what's made you restless your whole life."

Porter looked away, not wanting to hear this.

Emily continued, "Mary Ann says she thinks you also felt abandoned by Luana in the way of feelings. The reason she left you in her heart was because you were gone so much. I figure you already know that."

Porter looked at her and nodded slowly, rather surprised at her perceptions, and intrigued.

"Then after I got married each time and left you alone, you felt left again, by another person you loved. Once I figured this out, I still wanted to forget about you, but I just couldn't. I saw my last husband couldn't give up on his old mule, and it made me realize the missing piece of this whole puzzle. That happened just before he was killed."

"I'm sorry he died, Emily," said Porter. "I really am."

Through tears, she took her father's arm and held it as they continued sitting there facing the fountain.

"So the real puzzle to figure out," she said, "was not you, but me. No matter what you're like, or what I don't like about you, I am part of you, as you are of me, and I am cut out to love you no matter what stubborn streak I see that drives me crazy. Just like with that stupid mule."

"I appreciate the comparison," said Porter sarcastically.

"And I'm probably too much like you for my own good," she continued. "That's the hardest part of all this for me. But one thing I can tell you—I will never lose my love for you. I have tried—believe me, I have—but I cannot and never will, just as Mama never will, though she claimed otherwise."

"Claimed? What're you talking about?" said Porter, eyes wide.

I could see through Mama's claims, even as young as I was."

"What do you mean?"

"It's obvious she's never lost her love for you. Only she feared the future with you—and also not knowing about being left alone in the future. She was no different than many women. Mama will never love her new husband—just as she didn't love Alpheas. But they gave her what she needed for the moment. A steady feeling of knowing they'd be there every night."

Porter fought old feelings rearing up inside. "I didn't know she's had such a rough go of things since," said Porter, not knowing what else to say.

"Well I know a lot more about you now—and so does Mary Ann. I just saw her a few blocks south, heading home. I told her what I had decided and she cried a little and said she'd stick by your side no matter what. She has said that before, but this time she means it. A lot of what we have figured about you goes back to Joseph's teachings. I believe he said there are two kinds of sins—those by disobedience—and we've all disobeyed some way or another and we know what that's all about—but the other sin he talked about comes from tradition. Tradition, I believe, comes from that map that was written inside you by your folks and their folks and so on. But I think you're trying to settle down and rewrite those maps. All in all you've been as faithful to the Lord's kingdom as any man I could imagine, because you've always at least tried, and gone the extra mile for others, no matter what weaknesses and traditions were pulling at you. I think Mary Ann and I both see the rock you are, deep, deep down, below the traditions. And I believe it's your faith that put you there. I also think Joseph saw. I know Brigham does. And I know I do, too, Papa." Her eyes glistened as she then looked down. "I guess I just can't get away from the fact you're my hero. I can't."

Porter felt a ton of boulders lifted from his shoulders.

"Most importantly for me," said Emily, "is that I know I'm home."

Porter looked at her, then down for a moment, thinking. He knew that "from the mouth of babes" he had his answers. His own daughter had resolved the mystery, that for years had so haunted him, of why he had always felt driven to desert his loved ones. Furthermore, despite her overall optimistic assessment of him, he saw his own imperfections glaring him in the face, and knew he had to do something about it. He knew he had to devote his life—the time left in his life—to Emily, to Mary Ann, to his other children, and to every friend and soul in need with whom he'd come in contact who needed his time. He had lost Luana. He had lost Lot Huntington. He had a second chance, and he wasn't about to let that float away. Not for anything in the world. He kissed Emily on the forehead and gazed upward.'[8]

---

[8]   Porter Rockwell Chronicles, volume 4, Richard Lloyd Dewey, pp.553.

NEIGHBORS

There were beginning to be more raids by the Indians on the settlements. There were very seldom any whites killed, the Indians were hungry and so they only took food from the ranches. They were also upset because they had to take things that weren't theirs, but the whites had pushed them into it. They needed food to feed their families. Of course that wasn't the way the settlements saw it. They only felt the thieving Indians were at it again. Most whites thought the Indians were heathens with no morals. Few had made any effort to get to know them. A few had attempted to convert them, but maybe only to earn a better place in heaven. It seemed there was little concern about the Indians being real people. There seemed to very few who respected the Indians, perhaps Porter Rockwell and Ike Potter were pretty much alone in their respect for the Indians. Ike felt that connection to Porter, at least every time they talked that is what Ike walked away with. Ike still spent a lot of time with the Indians. He was beginning to feel a certain coolness by his neighbors. People who used to wave to him were beginning to look the other way. Every time that happened unusually it gave Ike a little laugh within. He always thought, well, I haven't changed, it must be you people who have changed. He also thought, well, at a time like this, I guess you find out who your real friends are. Maybe my real friends are in fact the Indians. These people are looking pretty flaky to me.

About that time one day Ike was thinking. He hadn't taken notice for awhile of Elmer Judd. He had known that he had the rank of a general in the Nauvoo Legion, which hadn't impressed him much, but when he realized he was now a bishop in the Mormon church and a judge, he thought, you have got to be kidding me. I hope he is smart enough to let the incident with Mary go away, but when he had gone down and had Mary sealed to him and her sisters, Ike suspected that there may be more problems especially now he was a general, a judge and a bishop. That is a lot of power in the hands of one man and he is a man who in Ike's opinion can't handle power.

Ike saw his mom in their yard and stopped for a chat.

"Are you keeping busy there, young lady," said Ike as he dismounted. "It seems every time I see you, you are slaving away. Can't you get any work out of that old man anymore?"

"Well, I think you call me young to make you feel younger, but then you totally blow it when you call your father old. They cancel each other out. I thought I had raised you to be a little smarter than that."

"Hey, here comes that old man around the corner now."

"You keep calling me old and you won't get any older. I'll see to that. You still can't whip me and you know it. I've always known the trick. When you suspect your kids might be able to take you, you quit wrestling with them and they never really know for sure, because the last time they tried it was to no avail to them. So I can still whip you. Are you ready to take that back or shall we go at it right here, in front of God and everybody."

"Well, I think I want to think about it for awhile," returned Ike. "You are pretty salty."

"You are darn tooting I'm pretty salty. If you ever doubt it, just come for a lesson."

"Not to change the subject, but did you know the General Judd, Bishop Judd is now a judge."

"Well, I had heard that and that seriously is a reason for concern. I think it is out of our hands, but I don't think he is a man to forgive and forget. The next time, I want you to give him your wife, alive or dead. This could be the ruin of you. Of course, I'm kidding, we would stand behind you no matter what and I didn't mean any disrespect for Mary or your love for her. We all still miss her and we always will. I'm just really glad we have Ike Jr. to remind us of a very special lady," said his mom. "I guess the whole thing is so absurd. I can't imagine what would possess any man to want the wife of another man. And to top it all off, it was after she had gone and for him to sneak down and have her sealed to him. You have got to be kidding. It is ridiculous."

"As ridiculous as the whole thing is, it just points to a ridiculous man. And if he can be that ridiculous, then he can be more ridiculous and not let it go. Now he has a lot of power, unbelieveable, I'm afraid we haven't heard the end of his ridiculousness yet. I am holding my breath for the next thing that will happen. Knock on wood, but I'm quite concerned. Why would he stop now, now he has a lot of power," said his dad.

"Well, if he needs opportunity, I guess my spending time with the Indians will give him some additional opportunities. I'm starting to feel some attitude from some of my neighbors. I hope it is just my imagination."

"It is not your imagination, but whenever it comes around to me. I am ready to deal with it. I have explained it so many times and I will never stop explaining it. You are one of the only men in this valley that doesn't ignore what is happening. We are robbing the Indian blind of all he has or has ever had and the biggest thing is their pride. I don't believe they really want to fight, but if your father saw me and the kids starving, you know he would do something about it, said his mom. "How far do they suppose we can push the Indian without them doing something about it. We were pushed so far in Ohio, Missouri, and Nauvoo and how we can forget about it. Maybe Brigham is partly to blame. He talks about how this land is ours and how we deserve it. Why do we deserve it, because he has named it our Zion. What about the people that beat us here and for thousands of years. Where is the sense in all of this? So you do, what you need to do and you know your father and I will be right here standing behind you. I could never be prouder of you than I am right now. You are standing up for what you believe in. Could there be a more noble thing to believe in and stand up for. It is very much like standing up for a child that is being bullied. Sometimes I compare you to Jesus Christ. You are fighting for what you believe in and your father and mother believe in the same thing."

PORTER'S INN AT THE POINT OF THE MOUNTAIN

Ike had an opportunity to stop past Porter's Inn one day. Most of his time was spent around Springville or in the mountains with his Indian friends. He seldom ventured this far north. As he stopped he hoped to happen into Porter that day. He stepped in out of the bright sun light. He was temporarily blinded in the dark inside of the Inn.

"Well, if it isn't that Indian lover, Ike Potter," yelled someone from far in the back.

"Yeah, it is, who has a problem with that, speak your piece?"

"I'm not looking for a tussle, mind you," said the voice. "As a matter of fact I'm a bit of an Indian lover also."

Then Porter Rockwell walked up and shook Ike's hand.

"I might have known it would be you, giving me a hard time. It's good to see you, Porter. Not that I see you too often."

"Well, I believe that is a fact. We are both far too busy, you with all your wives and me with rustlers and outlaws to chase. It seems like whenever I get down in your country I run into you up in the mountains cavorting with the Indians."

"Yeah, that is somewhat true. One of my wives ran off and went who knows where and another died. I guess I'm just too hard on women. What can I say? I'm down to two now and they are the cream of the crop and I believe I will stick with the two of them"

"When you say that women are tough to figure out, you are so right. I ran one off because I wouldn't stay at home back in Missouri. I hear she is in Minnesota now. My present one, Mary Ann, is always on my case about being gone so much. My daughter has run off to California three times and gotten married. She's tough on men too. She's lost all three of them, one to the fever and two to the Indians. When you figure out women, you look me up. If I'm in town, quite often you can find me right here."

"When do you figure the lid will blow off on this Indian situation," said Porter.

"I hate to say it, but any day now. All it will take is one big item and we will have all out war. Blackhawk and his band haven't yet lost their peaceful pattern, but it won't take much. One unfairness on the white man's part and it will blow sky high. We had a chance to settle the Indian problems peacefully, but that chance I believe is gone now"

As Ike rode back into Springville the sheriff had a warrant for his arrest. The nephew, Miller, of Judge, Bishop, and General Judd's had accused Ike of stealing his cow. He was held over night in jail and the next day was arraigned. Through the rest of the day and the early morning hours Ike had time to think things through.

Now, what had been exactly said that last conversation that Elmer and he had after Mary died. He had been so upset that day that Elmer had approached him about letting him be sealed to Mary. He still thought: the nerve of that man.

Elmer had said, "I curse you in the name of the Lord."

And Ike had said, "I curse you in the name of the dirty son of a bitch that you are."

Ike thought those were some strong words, but I would do the very same thing today. Just let me out of this place and I'll give him a piece of my mind again. After a little time Ike thought, maybe I better simmer down. That man has a lot of power now and I hope I don't continue to get caught in the middle of his ire.

Ike the next day was released due the fact that the cow was found.

Ike thought, if this keeps up, I will be busy just defending myself.

But Ike was right. That wasn't the last of it.

Every time a cow or horse was missing, Judge Judd sent someone to pick him up. Almost every time the case was dismissed due to lack of evidence. Ike knew if this kept up he wouldn't have a friend in the county. People are somewhat shortsighted when it comes to a man with a reputation and Ike was fast getting a reputation. Even if he was totally innocent it was looking like he was a thief. After one such event when Ike was given his freedom, his house and property were confiscated for the good of the people.

"Another 'cross—purpose' Judicial affair was consummated last night. The Probate Court of Utah County, the other week, sentenced "Ike Potter" to confinement in the penitentiary for appropriating other people's cattle to his own use, without the owner's consent. During the trial at Provo, the somewhat noted "BILL HICKMAN" arrived in great haste at court, as one of the prisoner's counsel, and urged the special plea that he, HICKMAN, had been authorized by Gen. CONNOR to make a grand treaty with the Indians south, and that POTTER, being an interpreter and a great man with the Indians south, was necessary in the conduct of said treaty. Therefore, the good of the Territory; and, in a degree, of the whole nation depended upon the immediate release of IKE POTTER from the grip of justice. The Court, however, "could not see it," and POTTER was accordingly ordered to the Penitentiary.

Rescue was then hinted, but the prisoner was given to understand that he would not be rescued alive. With that assurance IKE went with excellent grace to the lodgings aforenamed, doubtless partially consoled with the idea that, thanks to the jurisdiction conflict, a way of release would, soon become apparent, and that between ???? judicial stools, or rather benches, justice would ??? to the ground.

Nothing ??? was heard of the affair until last night when Judge BRAKE, having been applied to for a writ of ??? corpus, and having issued the same, sat in the Council house in this city, in Chambers, and ??? the ??? His Honor decided that the indictment was informal, being signed by fifteen Grand Jurors, while his critics insist that the foreman's signature alone is sufficient; that the property stolen was too indefinitely described; and that the location of the theft was too generally stated. POTTER, accordingly was discharged, to the general disgust of the non-stealing part of the community."[9]

Ike had now lost his property and moved to Star southwest of the Utah Valley. He later moved to Mona for a period of time.

Ike now had a reputation as a horse thief which was hard to accept. No matter what he did now, people had branded him as a thief and knowing it wasn't true was little consolation to him. He now spent more time with the Indians. He knew that his friends the Indians wouldn't turn their backs on him as the whites had.

[9] nytimes.com/1863/07/12/news/affairs-utah-conflict-jurisdicton-gentile-nomin...

THE BEAR RIVER MASSACRE

Ike had his problems. He had lost his home and his property when the court had confiscated them while he was in the penitentiary. He was feeling branded as a horse thief and he wasn't guilty of it, but Porter had his hands full also.

Several years before Porter had found a Shoshone girl in the north of the Salt Lake valley and had brought her back to live with the Neffs. The Neffs had taught her English and had named her Emma. Mary Ann, his wife later on, had spent a lot of time with her and had taught her not only English but a lot about their culture. Both the Neffs and Porter had become quite attached to her. She had later on wanted to go back to her people.

Porter had taken her back to the Shoshones, but he always wondered about her and how she was. On the trip back she had fallen from her horse and cut her upper arm severely. Port had done the best he could do, but he had known there would always be a scar where the cut had been.

"In January, 1863 word reached Salt Lake that a number of hostile chiefs, including San Pitch, Bear Hunter, Sagwitch, and Pocatello, had assembled several hundred braves on the Bear River north of Logan. The report said the Indians had built breastworks and dug rifle pits in a small canyon overlooking the river, and were challenging the white men to come and fight them.

Colonel Conner wasn't familiar with the area, so he hired Porter Rockwell as guide. The colonel didn't particularly want a Mormon guide, believing the Mormons were too sympathetic towards the Indians, but the colonel had no choice. None of his men were familiar with the Bear River country, whereas Rockwell knew the exact location where the Indians were fortified.

Port marked his X on the federal payroll book once again. His pay was $5 a day, plus expenses. Marshal Gibbs issued warrants for the arrest of the renegade chieftains, but when Port delivered them, Conner said he wouldn't be needing any arrest papers because he didn't intend on taking any prisoners.

The plan was a simple one. On January 22, 40 foot soldiers followed by two howitzers began marching north from Salt Lake.

Three days later four cavalry units led by Conner and Rockwell moved out, traveling at night only, hiding by day in settler' barns. They hoped that when the Indian scouts saw the 40 men on foot, the red men would remain in their fortifications, thinking they could win easily against 40 soldiers. The Indians wouldn't find out about the cavalrymen until the battle had begun.

Traveling at night in January was no easy task for the men with the horses. Many got frostbite during the first night's journey of 68 miles. Most of the men led their horses in an effort to keep warm. Port was wearing his heavy buffalo coat.

The Californians were tough, uncomplaining men. Most were eager to engage the enemy, even in winter. Port's respect for the volunteers increased with each mile of snowy road.

The plan worked. Thinking they had only a 40 man infantry to contend with, the Indians waited for the approaching soldiers, continuing to strengthen their fortifications.

There were about 75 Indian lodges in the ravine, some made of brush, but most of wagon canvas. The canyon opened up on a flat by the river, giving the Indians a clear view of the approaching enemy. The head of the canyon disappeared into the foothills, allowing a handy escape for the Indians should that become necessary. Both side approaches to the canyon were steep and rugged, providing difficult access for an approaching enemy, especially with snipers placed on the ridgetops.

The squaws had dug steps up and down the ridges and constructed willow rifle rests at strategic locations to increase their braves' accuracy.

Shortly before dawn on January 29, the cavalry passed the foot soldiers at Franklin, the nearest Mormon community. The mounted soldiers, under the command of McGarry, pushed their horses into the icy river. When companies K and M reached the west bank a sniper's bullet critically wounded one of the soldiers. Dismounting, the troopers scampered for cover behind bushes and rocks while some of the men hurried the horses back across the river so they could carry the approaching infantry across.

At sunrise a chief on a spirited pony appeared on the top of the breastwork. He waved his lance at the soldiers as he raced the pony back and forth. Other Indians waved scalps of white women on the ends of poles, trying to taunt the soldiers even more.

The troops charged just as the infantry reached the river. The soldiers had instructions to save their ammunition until they reached the top of the embankment. When the battle began, McGarry took some of the men to the north in an attempt to circle the area and attack the Indians from above.

The Indians had been waiting for this day a long time, and they didn't waste any time. The volunteers began to fall like flies. Conner was sick. Wounded and dying men lay everywhere. Many were suffering from frostbite and exposure in the sub-freezing temperatures. Unable to push into the withering fire of the Indians, the soldiers holed up behind bushes and rocks as the Indians picked away at them. Those trying to remove the wounded were shot too.

For about an hour it looked as if the Indians would be victorious. Then McGarry suddenly appeared behind the Indians to the north, with a clear field of fire from above. When McGarry and his men opened fire, the rest of the men below were encouraged, and charged up the canyon.

Caught in the crossfire, the Indians panicked. Some tried to escape into the forests above. Others headed for the river. For the soldiers, the battle became a turkey shoot. With dozens of the companions already killed or wounded by the

Indian sharpshooters, the soldiers didn't let up, even when they discovered there were nearly a hundred women and children running in confusion across the battlefield. With enthusiasm, they remembered Conner's order that there would be no prisoners.

Port climbed upon the breastwork to watch the slaughter. Initially he had fired at the Indians when it appeared they might whip the California volunteers, but when McGarry crashed in from the rear, changing the tide of the battle, Port had ceased firing. He knew the slaughter would be horrible, without any help from him.

Some excitement came in watching the running and shooting matches with the armed but desperate braves, but when there were no more warriors to fight, the soldiers began turning their attention to the women and children. Port was sick. Still, he stayed.

He noticed a group of women at the bottom of the draw. He wondered why they were crouching. They were doing something with their hands under their robes. Then he remembered Jim Bridger telling him that the squaws of some tribes, when taken captive by an enemy, would shove sand inside them so the enemy would find no pleasure in raping them. Port guessed that that's what these Shoshone women were doing, knowing they would soon be at the mercy of the California volunteers. Some of the women were carrying babies. Several older children were standing among the crouching women.

The scouting reports as relayed to Port hadn't indicated the presence of so many women and children. Had that been known, the battle plan might have been different, Port thought. Perhaps there could have been orders not to harm defenseless women and children. Port wondered if Conner had known about the women and children and just hadn't said anything.

Just when Port figured the battle would start winding down, two soldiers waded into the group of crouching women, smashing them with rifle butts. One young woman began running up the hill towards Port. There was something familiar about the way she moved, the way she looked.

The two men ran after and caught her, throwing her on the ground. One of the soldiers pulled up her dress and fell upon her. Port looked away, wishing he could interfere but knowing if he did the action would be considered taking sides with the enemy.

When he looked back, the man had gotten off the woman. Apparently the sand inside her had spoiled his fun. The soldier grabbed his rifle, and pushing the barrel against the woman's abdomen, pulled the trigger. The woman screamed, trying to roll away from the soldiers. The men were laughing as the second soldier fell upon the woman in an effort to rape her again, even as she was dying.

Port had had enough. After making sure his rifle was loaded, he raised it to his shoulder, Port thought he recognized something familiar in the woman's scream. Could it be Emma? Pushing the thought from his mind, he took careful aim with his rifle, hitting the first man in the side of his head, the second in the heart.

After taking a quick look around to make sure he didn't have to defend himself against someone who might have seen him, Port ran down the hill to the bleeding woman. At first he couldn't tell if it was Emma, the face was so twisted in agony. Then he saw the scar on her left arm and remembered the wound he had sewed up.

Port dropped to the ground, pulling her head onto his lap, brushing her hair into place, holding her close, calling her by name. She did not respond, though her screaming had ceased. A minute later she was dead.

Port raised his face towards the gray sky and offered a tearful prayer. He asked why life had to be so cruel, why the volunteers had to come from California, why the Indians had to raid emigrant trains, why the Mormons had to settle on Indian lands, why the mobs had driven the Mormons from Nauvoo. Where did it all begin? Where would it all end? Who was to blame? At least the two men who had killed Emma wouldn't be killing anyone else.

When Port stood up, the shooting had stopped. He thanked God the battle was finally over. He wanted to bury Emma, but the ground was frozen. He stretched her out straight on the ground, facing east. He straightened her clothing as best he could, covering the ugly wound and as much blood as possible.

While the soldiers rounded up horses, gathered up the loot consisting mostly of guns, ammunition and wheat, and looked after their wounded, Port headed back to Franklin to see about getting wagons and sleighs for the dead and wounded. He had to keep busy, not think about what had happened. He needed a drink of whiskey.

Before dark Port returned with ten sleighs to bring the wounded soldiers to Fort Douglas in Salt Lake. As the sleighs were being loaded Port mentioned to Conner that he was going back to Franklin to get more sleighs to carry the wounded Indians into town, where the Mormons could care for them.

"That won't be necessary," Conner said. "There are no wounded Indians."

Nearly 400 Indians were killed, including 90 women and children, making the Bear River battle the largest slaughter of human life in the history of the American West. Port saw 48 braves in one gruesome pile. One warrior had been shot 14 times.

Fourteen California volunteers had been killed, including two right at the end of the battle when their companions thought danger had passed. Forty nine were wounded, and 79 had frost bitten feet. Most of the men had gotten their feet wet in crossing the river.

The spoils included 75 horses, 70 lodges, 1,000 bushels of wheat. and large quantities of powder and lead.

Several months later Conner was promoted to brigadier general, but he was no hero to the Mormons, who had known many of the slaughtered Indians. The general feeling in Utah Territory was that a show of strength was necessary to turn back the increasing tide of Indian raids, but the indiscriminate slaughter of women and children had been uncalled for and unnecessary.

Upon arriving in Salt Lake, Port headed for the nearest saloon, hoping four or five square drinks might help him forget Emma."[10]

---

[10]   Storm Testament 6, Rockwell, Lee Nelson, pp. 420.

SPANISH FORK CANYON

After the Bear River Massacre, Porter was never quite the same. Whenever he was asked why he drank so much, his answer was, "I am trying to wash away all the blood I saw that day on the Bear River."

Porter had had his fill of Colonel Connor, now Brigadier General. He had no desire to lead him and his troops to any more Indian camps. He wasn't sure if it was the slaughter of the women and children or Connor's reluctance to help the wounded Indians who were left in the snow to freeze to death or die of their wounds before they froze to death. Either way there was nothing humane about the day and then to top it off, seeing Emma die the way she had. It would take a lot of whiskey to wash those memories away. There wasn't enough whiskey anywhere to solve that problem. Porter's memories of that day rode with him until his last day.

Then one day Connor approached him to lead him and his troops to an Indian encampment in Spanish Fork Canyon.

"Porter, I need your help again. I intend to deal with a Ute band in Spanish Fork Canyon and I would like to have you lead us there. Do you know where that band would be camped?" said Connor.

"I know exactly where they are camped, but you can forget me leading you there. That little journey to the Bear River was a little more than I can handle. Did you have to kill the women and children? Did you have to leave them dying in the snow to freeze to death?"

"I can't stand here and listen to that rubbish. I have a job to do and I intend to do it in the best way I deem possible. Civilians' opinions are of little importance to me."

"Well, if my opinion is of little importance then you need to find a guide that his opinion is of some importance to you. Ike Potter is your man. He knows where the Indians are to the south of here and I believe he will take good care of you," said Porter. "Good luck in your killing plans."

As Porter walked away, he thought about Ike Potter. If any man would take care of Connor it would be Ike. He knew exactly what Ike's sentiments would be about the Indians and the Indian problem. He and Ike had talked about the "Indian Problem" many times. He wondered exactly what Ike would do and he was anxious to see what that would be. He didn't think that Ike would just say no and let it go at that. He knew Ike would have something up his sleeve and he wondered just what it would be. Perhaps within a matter of days he would know that result. He was like a little child wondering with excitement how Ike would handle Connor and the "Indian Problem".

Connor wasted no time finding Ike.

"Ike Potter. You have been recommended to me to help me lead my troops into Spanish Fork Canyon. Do you have the time to do that?"

"I always have time for the federal government. I would like to congratulate you on your campaign into the Bear River country. I heard it happened just as you had hoped. There was narry an Indian left in the whole area to bother the settlements. Was there anything that you would have done differently if you had it to do over again?" said Ike.

"I sense a good portion of sarcasm in what you have to say. Do you not appreciate what the federal government does for you settlers?"

"No sir, I appreciate all the eastern leaders do for us. We should punish those people who were here for generations before us. What right do they have to stand in the way of progress? How dare they think they had any rights over ours. We are Manifest Destiny. It is our destiny to take away their lands and use it as we see fit. It is our right to kill all of their food supply so they beg in our streets. But no, I am totally willing to lead you to those rascals up in Spanish Fork Canyon. They have been stealing our cattle and scaring our women. Something had got to be done about them. I will meet you right here in the morning. Can you be ready at first light?" said Ike.

"I certainly can. My men are ready whenever they are given the orders to be ready. I will meet you here at first light."

Of course, Ike had no desire to let Connor get a chance to hurt his friends. Ike was off in a short while and rode all night to let Blackhawk and his band know what Connor intended. Blackhawk knew of the Bear River Massacre and he was quick to gather his people and move out of the canyon. Blackhawk thought of retaliating against Connor for what had happened in the north, but this was not the time or the place for that.

When Ike didn't show at the meeting place in the morning, Connor figured that he had been double crossed and he found a settler who led him up into the canyon. The settler was able to find where the camp had been and much to Connor's chagrin the camp was empty. When the troops rode into the Indian camp Blackhawk sat on his horse high above the valley and watched the soldiers. He knew what the troops would have done if they had found them in the camp. He had a small shudder go up his spine, but he knew his braves would have fought bravely.

When Connor got back into the valley he looked up Porter and told him what had happened.

"Rockwell, your man Ike Potter turned out to be a deceiver. He agreed to meet us the first thing in the morning and he never showed. When we found the enemies camp it was empty. I suspect your man Potter told the Indians we were coming. Is that the kind of man you recommended to me?" said Connor.

"Well, I know Potter knew the area and I was sure he knew where the Utes would be, but what he did from there was his doing. I can't control a man like that. I also suspect he was a friend of their's and there you have it. Sorry about the outcome. We can't always have ready Indians for you to slaughter like you did at Bear River. Good luck with your future campaigns."

As the troops rode away, Porter chuckled to himself. Ike Potter did exactly as I had hoped. I'm so tired of the senseless slaughter of the Indians. That Bear River incident will burn in my memory for a long time. I'll never be part of something like that again. Not ever.

Since he had had to think about Bear River again, he poured himself a stiff drink and hoped this one would remove the memory of Emma and how she had died. She had been such a sweet girl. How could he have changed what happened that day?

UTAH'S BLACKHAWK WAR

On Sunday, 9 April 1865, Ulysses S. Grant and Robert E. Lee met in the Appomatox Court House, Virginia, to end the Civil War. Both men were resolved of the outcome. The war had been fought for 4 years and the south had lost.

The very same day, a group of frontiersmen and a group of Ute Indian chiefs met outside of Manti, a small town in central Utah to avoid any more conflict. The winter of 64-65 had been usually severe and the Indians had been either begging in the streets or for those with too much pride to beg, there had been Mormon beef slaughtered. Present were Sow-ok-soo-bet, An-kar-tewets, Toquana, Blackhawk, and Jake Arapeen. John Lowry, an interpreter for the United States government Indian Office, had called the meeting after one of his cows had been slaughtered.

Lowry had been drinking and the negotiations went poorly. Harsh words were spoken and when Jake Arapeen notched an arrow, Lowry pulled him off his horse and proceeded to struggle with him on the ground. The chiefs who wanted peace separated the two, but negotiations were then over. Blackhawk and Jake Arapeen rode away yelling insults back at the frontiersmen.

Immediately Blackhawk moved his band away from the now defunct 12 mile creek reservation. The 12 mile creek reservation had been set up to try to teach the Indians how to farm. When the Indians were not able to maintain the reservation as the whites had hoped the reservation was closed to the Indians.

Blackhawk and his braves now began to gather Mormon beef and move his band and the cattle to the safety of Salina Canyon.

First blood of the Utah's Blackhawk Indian War was considered to be drawn when a group of young men riding north encountered Blackhawk and his braves moving cattle. The Indians fired on the youth and when the men turned back toward town Peter Ludvigsen fell from his horse with a bullet hole in the back of his head.

The Indians fell on the fallen Ludvigsen, smashed his face into a prickly pear, cut a large piece of skin from his back and ate it in a ceremonial opening of hostilities.

Ike Potter had hoped this day wouldn't come, but it was here. Blackhawk had gathered cattle and other bands on his way to Salina Canyon. He now had 125 animals and seventy men. Two Salina residents, Barney Ward and James Anderson unknowingly rode up Salina Canyon and were killed by Blackhawk's war party. Ike rode down into Salina Canyon and wondered if he would be killed also. As he rode into the camp several bows were raised but Blackhawk warned the braves off. Blackhawk and Ike sat down to talk.

"I had hoped this day would never come, but is it here now," said Ike.

"I'm afraid we have been quiet long enough. When Lowry treated us like animals a few days ago, it was too much. We are not animals and since the Mormons came here they have taken away our land, our food supply and now our pride. No man can continue to get this kind of treatment and do nothing. It was a very hard winter and what we used to have to make it through, is now gone. We beg in the town streets and there they treat us like animals.

I was baptized a Mormon, but I renounce that baptism and we fight. I, at first, led the Mormons against my people and I saw what the cannon fire does to us. I can't believe I did that, but I was hoping that we all could live together in peace. I saw the heads of my people displayed in the town square until they began to rot with mold. That is the people I had hoped to live in peace with. Now I know that is impossible. The Mormons made me chief and called me the friendly chief. They cannot make me chief. My people make me chief.

You, Ike Potter, are our only white friend and you will always be welcome in our camp. My sign today, to my braves, will always hold. You will be free to ride into our camp and ride with us as you always have."

Ike set up a location on the Oregon Trail and bought worn out oxen and horses as the emigrants came west. He rested them, fattened them up and resold them when they were ready to move on. It was a way to feed his family as the fighting continued in the Salt Lake valley. Ike tried to

stay out of the conflicts but he occasionally was riding with
Mountain or Blackhawk and found himself in the middle
of a skirmish. Ike felt torn by the events. He tried very hard
to keep his sentiments neutral. Most of his friends these
days were Indians, but he was white and he also knew of the
eternal punishment of the shedding of innocent blood.

John Walker and Charles Wilson started riding with Ike
at about that time.

During one of the skirmishes Squash Head was captured
and held in General Judd's house overnight. During breakfast
Squash Head, so named due to his flat face, cut his own throat
with a butter knife from ear to ear. Since Squash Head was
manacled it was severely suspect that he would have been able
to complete this feat. Sentiment was that a white man must
have killed him while he was so confined that night. Since
Squash Head had been accused of killing and cannibalizing a
white child little was done about the incident.

THE SALINA CANYON
FIGHT

Ike left Salina Canyon and rode home to check on the family. He loved to play with his children and he found home life near to heaven. He couldn't imagine anything nicer.

He was saddened by the choices his neighbors had made to turn against him. In his mind he always turned to, it was their choice. He guessed he had found who his true friends were. He was very saddened that all of this that could have been avoided had now turned into a full fledged fight. It could have been avoided. If the Mormons hadn't chosen to kill off the Indians food supply. The animals had been there for thousands of years and the Indians had never taken more than they needed and they had always left any area alone that needed to rebuild its supply. You never over use anything or it is gone and maybe gone forever. That is such a simple concept. Why couldn't the Mormons have figured that out. If they had used their heads and not taken more than that area would allow, it could still be as it had been for all time and all this fighting and loss of life could have been avoided. It saddened him to the depths of his heart that children were losing their fathers and would have to grow up without them on both sides. It hurt him to his very core to think of all the loss because people didn't stop and watch the custodians of this land, the Indians, and how they took care of this land. Now lives were being lost and the animals of the forest were lost and two cultures were totally at odds with each other and the only way to solve it now was to kill and it was now happening all around.

"Throughout 11 April, bands of mounted militiamen began arriving in Salina. Called out by Nauvoo Legion Colonel Reddick N. Allred, they came from Gunnison and such Sanpete Valley settlements as Manti, Ephraim, and Spring City. The following morning, 12 April, Allred started up Salina Canyon with a force of eighty-four men. Hoping the cattle could not taken over the canyon's summit on account of the snow pack, they planned to chastise the raiders and recover the stock. About fourteen miles up they came across freshly killed beeves, which apparently had just been abandoned in the process of being butchered. Certain the fleeing Indians must be just ahead, the troopers urged their horses through a narrow defile through which only one rider could pass at a time. Sometime after the last man had made it through the gap, and while they were strung out in a narrow gorge surrounded by steep canyon walls, they were attacked by a large native force concealed on the cliffs, horses bolted and reared as their riders dismounted and sought cover in the rocks and willows along the creek bottom. Still the troopers saw no Indians, only smoke rising from the rocks and trees above them.

Blackhawk's men poured down a "murderous fire" while the militiamen searched in vain for adequate cover or targets to shoot at. Sizing up their precarious position, Allred ordered a retreat. Immediately a panicked stampede of frenzied men and horses raced down the canyon "through Showers of balls like hail." In the confusion coats, saddles, blankets, and weapons were scattered as frantic horses threw their riders and went crashing through the brush. Once the untrained mass of men and horses started down the path, Allred found it virtually impossible to assemble them. He considered a rally necessary, however, because a number of his men were still up the trail under heavy fire. Jens Sorensen, a young Dane from Ephraim, broke his ankle when he was thrown from a mule, and he was shot in the hip as he hobbled towards his comrades. Several others near him struggled to free terrified horses whose bridles had become entangled in the brush.

The militia's retreat brought an estimated eighty attackers out of hiding. Simultaneously, Allred managed to rally twenty men, who for the first time returned effective fire, killing "two or three" Indians. By the time most of their straggling comrades reached the small collection of militiamen who remained with Allred, Ute cross fire dictated a second headlong dash for safety. As they fled, William Kearnes, the son of Gunnison's bishop, was shot in the head and killed instantly. Meanwhile, the wounded and horseless Jens Sorensen called on his fellows for help, but he was left to be killed, as "none had the hardihood to stay another minute under such fire."

The shooting during the ambush was so intense and the trap so well laid that most of the Mormons considered it a miracle that any of them escaped. One militiaman attributed their deliverance to two facts. First, Blackhawk's men "over-shot" their targets: "Had the Indians known how their guns were carrying they could have shot us down fast," he declared. Second, the raiders for some reason did not anticipate the legionaires' uncontrolled flight back to the gap and had stationed none of their men there. The panicked withdrawal of the majority of Allred's troops preserved their lives, and some of them later reminisced (with good reason) that had they not taken the pass so swiftly the outcome might have been similar to that suffered by Custer's men in 1876.[11]

When Ike heard the news he thought, "I know exactly where the ambush happened. They are so lucky that any of them survived. The gap where only one man at a time can pass through is so narrow. It was an excellent attack. I'm sure Blackhawk waited until they were almost all through the gap and then he attacked. That was a clever plan."

Sometimes Ike had a hard time picking a side in this conflict. He knew in his heart of hearts that this all could have been avoided and maybe he thought, "the whites are getting what they asked for. No people will be walked on forever. You have to fight for your families and what you believe in. What a noble cause to want enough food to feed your families."

---

[11] Utah's Blackhawk War, John Alton Peterson, p. 20.

THE BATTLE OF
GRAVELLY FORD

Ike heard that Blackhawk had been wounded and he rode to his camp in Salina Canyon. He found Blackhawk lying in his lodge in deep pain. Ike could see that Blackhawk wouldn't make it very long if he didn't get help. Ike thought he would find a better doctor in Manti than in Salina so he rode as quick as he could to look for one. He found a doctor in Manti that was capable of helping him.

"Doc, I need your help and if you can come as quickly as possible it would be appreciated. I'll tell you right up front. The man hurt is Blackhawk of the Ute tribe."

"How can you expect me to help a murdering Indian who has been responsible for the death of many of our friends and neighbors."

"You know Doc, the first time I asked you because you took an oath to help any human being. But now I can see you don't consider Blackhawk a human being, so I'm not asking anymore. It would be best for you if you get on your horse out front and move with me quickly to where he lies. I have no interest on using this gun on my side on you, but Blackhawk is my friend, probably a better friend than you ever could be and you WILL, come with me. You can come of your own free will or draped across that saddle. Either way, you are coming with me."

Ike and the Doc rode quickly to Salina Canyon. The braves let them through. They were used to seeing Ike. They quickly moved to Blackhawk's lodging. Blackhawk wasn't looking any better.

"You forced me to come here and now I'm not helping this man. You can't make me."

"The Indians have a treatment for people who refuse to do something that has to be done. They cut a little hole in their stomach and pull out their intestine about 30 feet and they can watch the coyotes eat their supper that night. I guess you probably can figure out how that would go. You are not leaving until you watch the coyotes eat or you save Blackhawk's live. If you keep refusing, it won't take us long to get the coyotes ready for supper. So make up your mind quickly. I'm not a doctor, but this man needs help. Make it snappy."

As the doctor worked Ike had a chance to ask how the battle at Gravelly Ford had gone. His Ute language was now good enough he could carry on a conversation quite easily.

"James R. Ivie and his relatives formed the nucleus of the village of Scipio and together owned large numbers of livestock. Various members of the Ivie family had played major roles in starting all three of the Mormon-Indian conflicts large enough to be termed "wars" that occurred before Blackhawk commenced his own. Richard Ivie, James's oldest son, it will be remembered, provoked the outbreak of the 1850 Fort Utah War when he, with two other Mormons, killed

"Bishop" in a squabble over a shirt and tried to hide the deed by filling the dead Indian's abdominal cavity with rocks and sinking the body in the Provo River. This event was viewed by the Utes as "the first blood shed" between Mormons and their people, and since as many as seventy Timpanogos Utes died in the subsequent fighting (which Antonga Blackhawk witnessed first-hand), it was never forgotten. James R. Ivie himself was credited with starting the Walker War in 1853 by hitting an Indian over the head with a gun. He played a less violent but equally effective role in precipitating the 1856 Tintic War, which resulted in the killing of Blackhawk's comrade Squash-Head and in the wounding of his friend and ally Tintic. It is therefore understandable that, since the large force of raiders found Warren Snow's home town of Manti "forted up," well guarded, and reinforced with militia from the north, Black Hawk would turn his attention to James Ivie's poorly defended Scipio. Finding Ivie tending to "a favorite milk cow" in a pasture within earshot of his door, the raiders raised the "war whoop," filled the old man with arrows, and stripped him of all but his boots.

Alarmed by the "war whoops" of Ivie's murderers, thirteen whites moved out towards the herd of 350 cattle and seventy-five horses the raiders had already gathered. They retreated, however, when fifteen Indians made a feint back towards the tiny village where the settlement's women and children were defended by five poorly armed men. Executing what was obviously an ambitious and well-conceived plan, Blackhawk drove the stock into a pass to the southeast. Called the "Scipio Gap," the pass provided a natural trail through

rough mountainous and broken hill country to the Sevier Valley and Blackhawk's oft-used escape route from there to Castle Valley and beyond via the Od Spanish Trail through Salina Canyon. Prepared to ambush and otherwise slow pursuers, as many as fifty Indians (who did not participate in the initial raid) were concealed on the trail near Scipio Lake to keep anyone from following. Similarly, another sixty warriors guarded the crossing at "Gravely Ford" on the Sevier River. Since it would take at least twenty hours to drive the stolen herd to the Sevier River, commanding the ford was necessary to keep Nauvoo Legion troops from cutting off the raider' retreat.

Once that raid was over, Scipio townspeople sent riders with calls for help to Nauvoo Legion brigades stationed at Fillmore and Gunnison. By 10:00 p.m. on 10 June Brigadier, General William B. Pace left Gunnison with all the troops he had at his disposal—a meager force of twenty northern volunteers supplemented by four of five local men. Assuming that the Indians would head the stock towards Salina Canyon, they traveled all night "through Mud and rain," reaching the deserted settlement of Salina about daybreak on 11 June.

Expecting reinforcements from Manti, Pace's command was disappointed to learn from five Sanpete couriers that help from the north was not forthcoming. Because Warren Snow and others viewed the raid as a feint "to attract attention from Manti," where "more serious depredations are contemplated," the Sanpete general opted not to weaken that settlement's defenses by sending additional men after Blackhawk; instead, he ordered his men to attend a military ball. Strengthened by only the five couriers, Pace's command saw about thirty Indians who were driving the stolen herd emerge from "the gap" just as the morning sun began to shine upon the west mountains. Ascertaining that the raiders were headed towards Gravely Ford, which lay three or four miles farther up the Sevier River near the present site of Vermillion, Pace and his thirty men quickly made their way to the ford. When they found it already in the possession of a force of sixty warriors, Pace "provoked an engagement."

Aware that his force was outnumbered at least three to one (counting the thirty Indians approaching the ford with the stock), Pace hoped to stall the herd on the west side of the river while he sent to Richfield for reinforcements. A three-hour gun battle ensued in which Pace and his men knocked "six or seven" Indians from their horses and "badly hurt" Blackhawk's "foot corp." Although bullets "fairly rained down" on them, the Mormons suffered only one minor casualty. At last Pace realized that his supply of ammunition could not sustain the battle much longer and ordered his men to retreat to a point just out of the Indians' range.

Realizing that the cattle could not pass until the whites were chased from the ford, "two or three" bold native horsemen sought to complete Pace's withdrawal by repeatedly riding close enough to fire at the militia. One of these horsemen, riding the white stallion formerly owned by the slain James Ivie, was clearly one of the raiders' head men. As the "white horse chief" swept by the Mormons again and again firing from behind his mount, Pace ordered his men to kill the beautiful animal. The horse was shot down at full gallop, but its body served its rider as a bulwark from which the determined Indian continued to fire. At last a Mormon sharpshooter hit the warrior in the stomach, and the militia men cheered as he retreated on foot "pressing his hands to his abdomen." A short time later, the militiamen left the Indians in possession of the ford and retreated.

As they withdrew, Pace's men noticed thirty distant riders emerging from "the gap" to the west. Unknown to Pace, the horsemen were Fillmore militiamen hurrying to come to his aid. The newcomers, strung out on the trail for a distance of two miles, looked like Indians to some of Pace's "Utah County boys." Even with telescopes the retreating troops could not make out whether the riders were Indians or whites. Aware that a force of thirty reinforcements with more ammunition could allow them to secure the ford and save the cattle, Pace's men debated for some time regarding the identity of the distant force. At last the general concluded that they must be Indians, believing there was no "man Holding office in the Legion so stupid" as to allow his men to spread out for such a distance while chasing a hostile force. Hence, he continued his retreat while the Fillmore troops watched in astonishment as the opportunity to save the large herd and punish the raiders slipped away."[12]

The "white horse chief" was Blackhawk and he was badly hurt. The doctor was able to sew up Blackhawk's wound and offer some pain remedy. The doctor wasn't sure what would

---

[12]   Utah's Blackhawk War, John Alton Peterson, pp. 270.

be the outcome, but he had done all he could. Ike believed he had and rode with him back from where he had taken him. Blackhawk was to live for 4 more years, not at his best, but at least he had been given a chance. A gut shot almost always means sure death.

COALVILLE

Ike was in Springville to see his parents and as he rode into town, he rode past his old property. Someone was living in the house he built and the barn he built for his animals. Life is funny how things can change. Apparently he messed with the wrong man. He wondered if Elmer was feeling good about getting even with him. He had altered his entire life. He also wondered if Elmer had any guilty conscience because of what he had done. He had to have a conscience, didn't he. There was the house that Ike built and here was the reputation that Elmer built. He was thought a thief by all of his old friends now. Whenever Ike thought this way he always came back to the idea, you find out who your true friends are. His Indian friends never turned their backs on him as the whites in Springville had. Well, he wasn't one to complain. He would just have to build his good reputation back. That shouldn't be that hard. Ike rode over to his mom and dad's.

"Hi guys, have you missed me."

"You have caused such a raucous around here, how dare you even show your face. This Blackhawk War that is going on, I'm sure it is your doing. If you weren't friends with the Indians this would never have happened. You must have spoiled them and they think they have more coming then they are getting. You must have caused this war," said Ransom.

"I want to kid Ike about all of this too. We all saw it coming, knew how to fix it and were ignored by all. But I bet Ike about now is a little raw about the whole thing," commented Rhoda.

"You know, I am. I've lost so much. My friends are the main thing I've lost. Other than you and my own family they were my most prized possessions. But I guess that says it all. People cannot be possessions. Friendships are at best tenuous. This has sure proven that to me. I have often thought when Christ was killed, probably his most hurtful thing was when his friends turned on him.

"You know we really don't blame you for any of this and we have been behind you in everything you have done. We know that you are not a killer. Sometimes you are there so you are thought of as part of the war on the Indians side, but we know the truth. We support you 100 per cent," said his mom. "Don't take this personal, but we are thinking of selling and moving out of here. We both like Coalville. What do you think of Coalville? We are a close family so we hope if we move there, that in time you will come there also. We already have an offer on our place."

"Well, there is no love lost in this place. I hate to say that. It was so important to me to have friends here and to be a good friend to all, but it is what it is. Sometimes it is best to move on. It would be closer to my business up on the Oregon Trail. I would be gone less time. It is almost a day's ride farther here than to just stop in Coalville."

They moved all of them to Coalville. Ransom used a dugout he found in the banks of the Weber River.

Ike contracted to move 4500 pounds of grain to Fort Bridger. As he started up the road to Fort Bridger he was a bundle of thoughts. He didn't want any more of his Indian friends killed and he didn't want any more whites killed. He wanted this war over. He had a thought what if he used this grain to try to solve the conflict. If he could use this grain to get food for the Indians and get the whites to show good intentions maybe all could be solved. Maybe this war could be ended. Could he use this grain in some way to ransom food for the Indians and stop the war? For now he would hide the grain and decide what to do next with it. He would in the end make sure the owner of the grain was restored with the value of the grain.

"In 1866 Judge Bean and his friend Bishop Johnson exacted revenge on Ike Potter. "We sold him out of house and home at Provo for selling liquor to Indians and hiring them to steal cattle. Now homeless, Ike went to Coalville, where his father, Ransom, was living below the town in a dugout on an island in the Weber River.

Many in the Coalville area viewed with alarm the presence of Ike Potter in their town. In October 1866, several prominent men of Coalville met and formed a resolve to be rid of Ike Potter. Those at the meeting were: Jacob Hoffman,

Jackson Redding, William Smith, Charles Livingston, Dick Eldredge [sic], and Joseph Brim. They bided their time until the opportune moment came to strike. All the while stories of Ike Potter and his gang flew through the Mormon populace.

Sometime after the beginning of the Blackhawk War, Indians told Mormons that Potter and his men instructed them 'to go down to Sanpete, and gather up a large lot of the horses and cattle there and drive them down East. And, they would be there and trade the horses and cattle to emigrants, and get them money, tobacco, whiskey and horses that would be their own. So, they went and got the horses and cattle, and drove them where the men wanted and the men sold them the way they said.'

The following summer, Potter was described by whites at the Uintah Agency as having been drafted as 'War Chief by angry Utes, and along with a handful of white ruffians, he was frequently seen with Black Hawk's brother, Mountain, and sometimes with Black Hawk himself. That same year, the extent of Potter's involvement with the raiders began to come clear, as Mormons learned that 'four whites' were 'coleaging' with the raiders. Ike Potter was suspected of being with the Indians in June 1866, at the battle of Thistle Valley in Spanish Fork Canyon. There, Black Hawk's men fought a pitched battle with a force of Mormon Militia....

In the spring of 1867 Ike Potter was again in trouble. Stephan Nixon gave Ike on March 4th an assignment of 45 sacks of grain to be delivered to the army at Fort Bridger, Wyoming. Ike didn't deliver. Instead he stowed the assignment in Cache Cave, a large cave in Echo Valley. Nixon, worried about the fate of his grain, filed suit on May 3 for non-delivery and had another man go get the grain. Ike was ordered to pay $135.90 plus court costs. The consensus in the valley was that Ike had tried to steal the grain, as there is no other explanation as to why he didn't fulfill his contract.

Near the end of June 1867, Ike, accompanied by Chief Black Hawk's brother, Mountain, showed up at the home of Coalville's bishop (mayor) William W. Cluff. Potter and Mountain claimed that they represented Chiefs Tabby, Sowiette and other reservation Indians. They demanded 15 beefs and a lot of flour.

The mayor and other Coalville settlers gave the two very little. Cluff wrote to President Brigham Young, "Potter is part of an organized band of thieves that steal stock from the residents, travelers and … coal haulers…. They had infested the area for a long time, call themselves Latter-day Saints and had frequently been arrested but because of their cunning they evaded the law…. The request by Potter was simply a scheme to give him greater influence with the Indians."

It was probably at this meeting that Mountain grabbed the mayor's hat and began taunting him. "An Indian pulled his hat off, raised it on a pole in the middle of the street and a war-dance was had around it." However, Cluff kept his cool and told them that he could spare only one beef and a little flour and that was it. Piqued, Potter and the Indians rode off.

Seeking revenge, shortly after the incident with Cluff, the Indians made an attack on a sawmill on Chalk Creek,

15 miles from Coalville. Two Indians were killed and two Mormons slightly wounded. Dispatches as to the incident read, "Ike Potter, a notorious renegade white man, was the principal leader of these Indians."

During the next few weeks several incidents occurred that, though hard to place in precise chronological order, were significant to the saga of Ike Potter. The time was ripe for the Coalville Conspirators to strike. The opening gambit was a rustling charge....

Jacob Huffman (Huffman,) one of the conspirators, claimed that he had found where an animal had been killed on July 20 about 200 yards from Ransom Potter's dugout home on his Weber River Island. Mr. Wheaton, a neighbor, was missing a lame-footed red and white ox. August Nelson would testify that he was camped near Ransom Potter's house the night of July 19. The next morning, just before sunrise, Nelson saw a man drive a red and white ox of four or five years old from the hills and put it in Potter's corral. Then Ike Potter and another man, Charles Wilson, put a rope on the animal, and Wilson led while Ike followed as they took the ox to the river. A shot was then fired. A key witness to the happening, John Y Greene (Green), who could testify as to the identification of the animal, never showed for the upcoming trial.

Ike Potter felt it was a bad rap. When word reached him that he and two of his sidekicks, Charles Wilson and John Walker, were to be charged with rustling, the trio took off for Fort Bridger to get help from the soldiers at that post.

On the way to the fort, Potter and his pals met a group of miners headed for Coalville. Andrew Miller, one of the miners, related that at this meeting Potter said "that the people of Coalville accused them of stealing and they were going to Bridger to ask protection from the soldiers. If they could not get it there they would call in Black Hawk and clear out Coalville." The story as told and enlarged upon in Coalville caused considerable apprehension.

Potter got no help at Fort Bridger. He did get a letter from the post commander, Lt. Col. Amon Mills that was found in Ike's pocket after he was murdered. Col. Mills' letter read: "July 26th, 67. I have just received your note. If you are charged with any crime and are pursued the best thing you can do is to come in and surrender yourself to Judge Carter and let the law run its course. No one shall do you any unlawful harm if I can prevent it."

When Ike Potter left Fort Bridger he sent a letter to his father, Ransom, back at Coalville. The mail carrier was John Y. Greene, the same man that would fail to show up and testify at Ike's rustling trial. The story around Coalville was that Greene "intercepted" a letter between Ike Potter and his father. How a man sworn and paid to deliver the mail can intercept a letter is beyond me. But then again during the years of the Reformation, little escaped the All-Seeing Mormon Eye.

The letter, of which no copy has been found, was produced at the investigation after the death of Ike Potter. Bishop Cluff would testify that the letter stated "that he (Potter) had just received a letter from Colonel Mills who promised to protect him and that if the damned Mormons hurt him, he, Mills, would send them all to hell the damned sons-of-bitches."

About this time, Potter and his gang powwowed with a group of Indians on the Bear River. Supposedly, Black Hawk was with this group. The Indians later reported that Ike Potter with eight to 10 other white men rode into their camp on Bear River and wanted the Indians to go to Coalville with them. Potter said they were going to have some fun. The Indians thought there would be trouble and refused to go. Potter told them that if they would go with him they would have all the beef, mutton and whiskey they wanted. In this manner, Potter was able to recruit six or seven Indians.

Ike Potter had put the fear of the Lord into the people of Coalville. J.C. Roundy, the Summit County sheriff, had a warrant for the arrest of Potter, Wilson and Walker for the rustling of Wheaton's ox. But when on the afternoon of July 28, 1867, word reached Roundy that Ike Potter with 15 white men and some Indians was camped on his father's island below town, the sheriff felt it prudent to form a posse to serve the arrest warrant.

Deputy Sheriff Hawkins called for help on Capt. Alma Eldredge of the Coalville Cavalry (Mormon Militia.) Eldredge and his company (about 13 men) accompanied Hawkins and sneaked up on and surrounded Ike Potter and his gang. "Four men were tapped for the job of exterminating Potter and his gang, Chester Staley, John Staley, William H. Smith and Alma Eldredge, all known to be accurate riflemen."

Apparently, Ike Potter and his gang didn't know that they had been sneaked up on as nothing happened that night. The next morning John Staley walked into the outlaw camp, served the warrant and accepted the peaceful surrender of Potter, Wilson and Walker.

The indictment was read before Judge George G. Snyder. The trio pled innocent and was released on bond and the trial set for July 31.

As previously noted, at the trial on the 31st, the conspirators' main witness, the mailman John Y. Greene, didn't show. Because of this, the case was continued until August 10. The prisoners were again released on bail.

The conspirators were frantic. Their pigeon was about to fly the coop. A man was sent galloping to Salt Lake City to get the help of the Danite Arza Hinkley. The conspirators got Isaac Shaw on behalf of his business partner, Williams, to allege that he also had a missing cow stolen by Potter, Wilson and Walker.

On August 1, Potter, Wilson and Walker came to the courthouse to answer to the new charges. Because Judge Snyder had an ongoing case, they were remanded to jail until the next day. Joshua Wiseman and James Mahoney were to guard them in the rock school building. The pigeons were back in the coop. Now, if only Arza Hinkley would get there in time.

Midnight, from the north hooves pounded down the main street of Coalville. Ten grim men reined in before the rock school. The door was kicked in. Wiseman and Mahoney scurried to one side. "Come out!" barked Arza Hinkey. The story as told by Judge R. N. Baskin:

"Isaac Potter, Charles Wilson and John Walker, residing at Coalville, were apostate Mormons. Walker was a boy about nineteen years of age. These three persons had previously been arrested for alleged thefts, and in every instance had been discharged by Judge Snyder, who at the time was probate judge of Summit County. In August of this year, they were again arrested on the charge of having stolen a cow. While they were under guard in the schoolhouse at Coalville, ten persons, armed, appeared about twelve o'clock at night at the building and ordered the prisoners to leave. Upon reaching the street they were placed in single file, a short distance apart, and in each intervening space two of the armed persons placed themselves. The others took positions at the front and rear of the procession thus formed. In this order they marched along the principal street of Coalville, through the mainly inhabited part of the town. Arriving at the outskirts, and their captors continuing to move on, Potter turned around and said to Walker: `John, they are going to murder us! Wouldn't you like to see your mother before you die?' Thereupon one of the armed men marching behind Potter thrust the muzzle of a shotgun against Potter's mouth. Potter in terror, shouted `murder!' Whereupon the armed man discharged the gun against the body of Potter at a range so close as to cause his instant death. At the discharge of the gun, both Wilson and Walker broke away and ran for their lives. Wilson was overtaken and killed at the edge of the Weber River. As Walker made his escape, a charge from a shotgun grazed his breast and lacerated his hand and wrist. He was wearing neither coat nor vest, and the charge set his shirt on fire and as he ran he extinguished the fire by the blood from his wounds. He was an athletic youth and soon distanced his pursuers. Although a number of shots were fired at him in the pursuit, he reached the river without further injury, swam across, and thereby escaped assassination. After numerous hardships he succeeded in reaching Camp Douglas, where the commanding officer, upon hearing what had taken place gave him support and protection."

Ike Potter lay dead on the main street of Coalville, a gaping wound in his chest, in blood atonement, his throat slit from ear to ear. His 10-year-old son, Charley, looked down and three times called his father's name. He then would have taken his father home but was prevented from moving the body by men who would later say that no one claimed Ike Potter's body. The outlaw was buried face down outside the cemetery north of town.

Later, a dam covered the burial site. Still later, during a low-water year, the bones washed up at "Potter's Point," and for years were displayed in the Summit County sheriff's office. They were finally buried in an unmarked grave in the Provo, Utah, Pioneer Cemetery.

Word of the murder was leaked to the gentile judge, John Titus. There were to be hearings. The two principal government witnesses were the escaped John Walker and a man known only as "Negro Tom."

John Walker hung around Fort Douglas, letting his wounds heal and awaiting time to testify. Someone slipped him a note, "Your mother is deathly ill. Come immediately." He never made it to Coalville. He was never heard from again.

Negro Tom, who had been brought to the Territory by the Mormons as a slave, and lived many years in the family of Brigham Young and other dignitaries called upon some Federal officials and stated that he could give important evidence in regard to some of these murders. A few days after, his body was found upon the 'bench' two miles east of the city, horribly mangled, his throat cut from ear to ear, and on his breast a large plaque marked: "Let White Women Alone."

In all such cases of assassination, Mormons can command abundant evidence that the victim has 'insulted a Mormon woman.' Thus the best witness of these crimes was removed, and the proof put beyond the reach of earthly courts.

Hearings were held before Judge Titus, but as the key witnesses were gone there was no testimony of substance. The guards Wiseman and Mahoney said that Potter and the others tried to escape and that they shot at the fleeing prisoners but didn't think they hit them. Bishop Cluff said that, accompanied by John Y. Greene, he left town about midnight to amputate the leg of a boy and didn't get back until after everything was over. All the other men of Coalville testified that when the shootings occurred they were home in bed. They mocked the judge and got away with it. The Danite Arza Hinkley was installed as probate judge of Summit County. And that was the end of Ike Potter, the father of Lava's first permanent settler."[13]

---

[13]   http://wilsonpioneers.blogspot.com/2010/04/potter-family.html

MARY ANN

On September 28, 1866 Mary Ann died, two weeks after giving birth to her sixth child. Porter hired a house keeper, Christine Olsen. Two months after Mary Ann died Porter sold his Inn at the point of the Mountain and purchased the Colorado Stables between south temple and first south. Porter later on married Christine Olsen.

Porter's marriage to Christine resulted in three daughters. Porter while at his Colorado Stables laid down with chills. The next day he slept until late afternoon. He sat up with a start, pulled his boots on, and fell back into the bed, Porter Rockwell was dead. It was June of 1878.

EPILOGUE

Issac Smith Potter

Ike Potter, was he a hero or a villain. Rumors spread like wildfires and it has proven to ruin the lives of people before. Gossip, rumors are little more than gossip and where do they stop. Have you ever played the game where a comment is made and it spreads around a circle of people? When you get to the end of the circle what was began has taken on a totally different meaning.

But we here are not talking about a comment going around a circle of people. We are talking about ruining the life of one man and in the end taking his life. Did it all begin with Elmer Judd and his jealousy? Did one man start rumors to avenge his not getting his way with a dead woman. A woman who was as dearly beloved by her husband as any woman could be. Ike mourned the death of Mary to the point of obsession. Aseneth mourned the death of Mary to the point of obsession. As the author wrote the part of how crazy Ike was about Mary of how much he was in love with Mary, he felt a very warm feeling come down over his shoulders. Was that Ike's spirit approving of what was being said? Those who believe in the afterlife, that spirits can come back and visit us, will readily feel that that was in fact Ike letting the author know that that was exactly how he felt about Mary.

Occasionally we get a chance to commune with the departed and what a great experience to know Ike approved of what was being said.

Elmer thought in the next world Mary should be in his sealed family because she had two sisters in that union. Where and when do we give people a chance to choose for themselves. The author hopes Mary is now happy and content and all of this is not now agonizing her any longer.

We don't know if Porter and Ike were good friends or if they were only acquaintances. We do know that Porter knew Ike well enough to know exactly what Ike would do the day he was approached by Colonel Conner to find the Utes in Spanish Fork Canyon. He knew Ike would never lead the troops for a slaughter in that canyon as he had in the Bear River Massacre. Porter never knew if he resented most the killing of the women and children that day or the leaving of the wounded Indians to freeze to death in January of 1863. Either way he knew he could never respect any man that would do what Colonel Conner did that day. Porter had not known that day what Colonel Conner's intentions were otherwise a reasonable person would assume that Porter would not have been there.

Ransom Potter, Ike's father, tried for 10 years to have the murderers punished for what was done to Ike, Charles and John. Each time the judge would say and where are your witnesses to what happened. Of course, Negro Tom was found dead, accused of something he probably didn't do and John disappeared never to be found. Each time the judge had to say "Dismissed for lack of witnesses." Ransom as late as 1877 was still trying to have those men punished for their actions.

Was Ike Potter an apostate? Ike's reputation had been ruined. When a man who is a Bishop, a General in the Nauvoo Legion and a Judge continues to accuse a man of foul deeds, people begin to think he is guilty. If he attended church meetings would people stare? Quite possibly and to think that Ike could keep attending his meetings when his reputation was ruined makes reason stare. In his heart Ike never apostatized. Ike was sealed to 4 women and he knew the principles of the gospel. Ike's ruined reputation preceded him to as far away as Coalville. Ike's choices were limited and in the end, his life was limited.

ORRIN PORTER ROCKWELL

Porter Rockwell, hero or villain. Porter's parents lived in a cabin near the Smith's home in New York. Porter and Joseph Smith became fast friends. Although Joseph was several years older than Porter they shared a limp when they walked and that gave them a reason to feel connected. Porter served as Joseph Smith's bodyguard and later after Joseph's death as Brigham Youth's. Porter his entire life regretted not staying with Joseph Smith the day he was martyred. He felt that maybe he could have stopped his death.

As a youth Porter was a timid farm boy. As a man he was still timid. That was all stopped when he was forced to stay in an out-house while his family was terrorized as the roof was torn off his home with Luana and the children inside by Missouri mobsters bent on driving the Mormons out of the area. Porter vowed from that day forth to never again be unable to defend himself or his family. He found a gunfighter that prepared him to become one of the most capable gunfighters in the West. He never received the acclaim that others such as Wyatt Earp and other sheriffs received but none the less he was one of the best with a gun in the Old West.

He was a sheriff in the Salt Lake area and therefore had to bring many men to justice. Porter Rockwell was a good man. He felt all the emotions of love and caring that other men feel, but he had a hard job to do that left him in situations where the taking of another's life was sometimes required. Porter never enjoyed the taking of another's life. He only took a man's life when there was no other choice. It was always a situation of kill or be killed.

AUTHORS NOTES

I am Ike's great, great grandson and I intensely resent another man wanting Ike's wife. Elmer is now recorded in the records as being sealed to Mary Ford. Ike also is recorded as being sealed to Mary Ford. Elmer was married to 13 other women, two of them being Mary's sisters. Does that give a man reason to hound a man to his grave? Ike now has a marker on his grave in the Provo, Utah's Pioneer Cemetery.

DISCLAIMER

Some of the names have been changed to protect the innocent. This book has no intention of hurting any of the family of those who did wrong during those days of hard men and women. It took hard men and women to carve out of this wilderness what we have today and we will be eternally grateful for all they did. Hopefully the families of those who murdered Ike can be at peace with something they had no control over. Hopefully the families of the Indians can also rest in peace and not be haunted by the injustices of this period in history.